I0642076

Margaret W. Evans

Theatrical Sketches

here and there with prominent actors

Margaret W. Evans

Theatrical Sketches
here and there with prominent actors

ISBN/EAN: 9783337096120

Printed in Europe, USA, Canada, Australia, Japan

Cover: Foto ©Andreas Hilbeck / pixelio.de

More available books at **www.hansebooks.com**

THEATRICAL SKETCHES

HERE AND THERE WITH
PROMINENT ACTORS

BY

MARGARET

" For they are the abstract and brief chronicles of the time."

CONTENTS.

ILLUSTRATIONS.

THEATRICAL SKETCHES.

Lester Wallack Averse to the Stage. His Advice to a Young Lady.

A YOUNG girl received some advice from the late Lester Wallack one evening that seemed somewhat surprising in view of his lifelong association with theatricals. I must first, however, relate a comical prelude.

The young girl referred to was invited to dine at the house of a friend, without having an idea of whom she was to meet. The hour appointed for dinner was seven.

On the night designated the rain descended in torrents, and the carriage which was to take her to dinner did not make its appearance until ten minutes before seven. When it drew up before her door it proved to be a covered landau, into which the young lady, clad in long cloak and pink silk hood, hastily entered, directing the coachman, as she did so, to drive at the top of his speed.

The coachman obeyed orders, and as they swayed over the car tracks from one side of Broadway to the other, the roof of the landau suddenly unlocked and fell open, leaving the young woman exposed to the storm. There was no time to lose, so, without disturbing the driver, she opened her umbrella and sat calmly up in her large open carriage, the observed of all observers.

Arriving at their destination the coachman was greatly surprised on becoming aware of what had occurred "behind his back," but not stopping to bandy words the girl ran quickly into the house and disencumbered herself of her damp outer garments.

As she entered the drawing-room she

found thirteen persons awaiting her.
Foremost among them was Lester
Wallack, his monocle in his eye, and a
quizzical expression behind it. "Well,
young lady," he remarked, "for the
youngest and smallest of the party you
are doing remarkably well. We await
your pleasure," at the same time making her a sweeping bow.

Though the position was one to cause
an older heart to quake, the girl decided
to "go in" with a dash and make the
best of it, and accordingly described her
late experience with such humorous real-
ism that the guests, who also included
the late Dion Boucicault, were more than
mollified and amused. At the close of
her recital Wallack ejaculated, "Brava!
little one ; well done around ; there'll be
the making of a good actress in you some
day."

At the dinner table, however, Mr.
Wallack gravely set to work to disabuse
her mind of the idea.

"But are you not fond of your profession, Mr. Wallack?" asked she, in some surprise. "No," replied Wallack, "I detest acting and always have. Never allow yourself," he added, "to be persuaded to adopt the life. A man may be able to stand it, but absolutely the stage is no place for a woman, and more particularly when the woman happens to be a lady."

At the same dinner the conversation having turned upon stageland in general, and prevailing salaries in particular, Dion Boucicault remarked in his unctuous brogue, "Ah! but the youngsters now-a-days prefer grumbling to working; no matter for his qualifications, each one seems to be satisfied with nothing less for his recompense than the salary of a 'leading man.'" Continuing, he said: "What could they have made of the old days, I wonder, when it sometimes cost a young buck anywhere from £1 10s. for the honor of walking as Hamlet's ghost, £1 to preside as first grave-digger, and so on, in proportion?"

The smallness of Mr. Boucicault's appetite then became a subject of remark, as such personal matters will, in the case of distinguished persons, large cups of black coffee seeming to take the place of the usual courses. When appealed to, Boucicault acknowledged that he ate comparatively little, working and existing largely upon black coffee.

The talk veering round to "properties," costuming etc., Boucicault was asked where he had raised the outfit so truly appropriate that he had worn as Con in "The Shaughraun." At this he indulged in a smile, called forth by some amusing reminiscence, accompanied by that inimitable twinkle of merriment that was never long absent from his eyes. "And well may you inquire," he responded, "for I had been so busy with the rehearsing and setting of the piece that, up to within a few days of its production, I was in as blessed a state of ignorance as to what me own trappings would be as you were likely to be yourselves ; but as it finally occurred to me that I'd have to wear *something*, I explored the trunks and closets containing the old stage wardrobe at Wallack's, and I finally fished out a disreputable red coat, formerly the property of John Brougham, so I just borrowed it for old acquaintance' sake and I had never another one to me back during the entire run of the piece."

In reference to Mr. Boucicault as an author, it is a fact that for many years there was never a night but that one or other of the four hundred and odd plays which this wonderfully clever man had originated or adapted was being presented in some portion of the English-speaking world.

A Glimpse of the Domestic Life of Edwin Booth.

THAT part of the community who only knew the late Edwin Booth as our country's most celebrated actor would probably have experienced surprise had they obtained a glimpse of his domestic life with the second Mrs. Booth—to have witnessed the meekness of manner, you might say, with which he complied with her suggestions. That last, however, is scarcely the word for the place, as she was usually in the imperative mood.

The Mrs. Booth I refer to was one of the most extraordinarily small and precise of women, and it was difficult for the observer to discover wherein lay her attraction for the great actor, likewise her claim to such absolute control as she practised over her family.

As an instance of the latter I may cite the following, which occurred nightly, and with absolute regularity, at a summer resort where a number of people, including the Booths, were passing a part of the season.

Miss Booth would possibly be engaged conversing with some of her acquaintances, Mr. Booth immersed in a book. On the stroke of ten, Mrs. Booth, with index finger pointing dramatically at the clock, would enunciate warningly the single word—

" Edwina."

Without an instant's hesitation, Miss Booth would bid her friends good-night and retire.

In possibly half an hour's time, Mrs. Booth, in the same warning voice, would remark :

" Mr. Booth."

Booth, glancing dreamily up from his book, would regard the small lady for an instant as if gradually collecting

EDWIN BOOTH in "Hamlet."

himself from some other sphere, and then, as obediently as Edwina, he would gravely bid good-night to those present, and likewise retire.

All his life Mr. Booth seems to have evinced a general desire to evade notoriety, except that which came to him through his legitimate profession.

There probably never existed a time, after his fame as an artist was established, when he could not, had he so desired, have been the social lion in whatever portion of this great country he chanced to be. But countless inducements were but proffered him in vain ; he seldom gave them very much heed, and only seemed really to *live* while upon the stage.

As a young man, he would receive notes of adulation almost by the bushel basket from the fair ones who could no longer mask the feelings he inspired in them, but they were rarely even perused ; in fact, I fear the only answer-

2

ing emotion they called forth was one of contempt.

In his life there was just one house in New York where the great actor could be induced to spend a social evening; and yet, so far as he was concerned, you could scarcely term it that, for the reason he frankly gave for coming was that his hostess allowed him to do as he pleased; which was to listen to the good music usually provided and of which he was very fond, to wander about the rooms watching and studying the faces and actions of those present, and above all not to have introduced to him any of the numerous guests who were but too eager to exchange a few words with "Edwin Booth."

In fact, it was curious to contemplate this silent, rather melancholy, dark-eyed man, to whom every one wished to pay court, persistently denying himself to them; who was sometimes moving in the throng, but never of it.

The History of an Unproduced Play.

Is there another profession or business so productive of uncertainty and " hope deferred," as that of the play-wright? A play may seem to possess, and be acknowledged to have every re-quisite for success, and yet, for reasons unaccountable, it may never see the light of day, or, more correctly speak-ing, the glare of the footlights. With this and other knowledge, it is frequent-ly amusing, though, in the case of a person interested, sometimes irritating as well, to be regaled with the ideas of those who have not pierced the intrica-cies and bewildering unexpectedness of the dramatic maze. The latter will speak of " writing a play," and " taking it to this or that manager for produc-

tion," as though " A, B, C,"were com-
plex by comparison.

For the benefit then of the uninitiated,
I will recount the adventures, from its
inception up to date, of one play coming
within my experience. An unproduced
one as yet, though meantime, possibly,
hundreds of others may have been
brought before the public containing
not one-sixth of its claim to interest and
consideration.

In this instance an adverse fate seems
to be the only feasible explanation, still,
it is difficult to determine.

A few years since, Miss Marie Wainwright, Mr. Louis James and a friend
of theirs, a playwright, were engaged one
afternoon in an animated conversation
relative to the writing of plays, the sub-
jects of superlative interest for the
plots of the same, and that most un-
certain of all quantities, the "public
taste." They happened at the time to
be seated in Miss Wainwright's parlor

at the " Gilsey House" (New York), and the discussion waxing strong at the point of the selection of plots, the actress rose, and picking up a volume from the centre-table, handed it to the play-wright suggesting the reading of it without delay, and adding that while it was not necessary to make an adaptation of it, which indeed would hardly be possible for the American stage, that it was, from her point of view, one of the most exciting and dramatic French novels she had ever read, and, in any event, could not fail to suggest unique ideas to the author.

The latter accepted the book, and followed Miss Wainwright's advice in reading it almost immediately, and, after careful consideration, decided upon the combination of some original ideas made possible by the story, and a certain number of those contained in the book, feeling assured thereby of a more than

ordinarily strong foundation upon which
to build a play.

After some months of labor the work
was completed and ready for inspection,
when its travels commenced, and sy-
nonymously the trials of the author.   At
the suggestion of Mr. Arthur Wallack
(the late Lester Wallack's eldest son),
who happened to be the first to peruse
the MS., certain portions of the piece
here and there were revised, and after
this was accomplished, Mr. James W.
Morrissey's was the first managerial
ear to be engaged in a hearing of the
same.

Nothing could have been more satisfactory or encouraging than his enthusiastic expressions and criticisms in
regard to it.   He formulated various
plans for its production on the instant,
subsequently making most vigorous
efforts to realize them ; but they were
not destined to be successful, and meantime the playwright one morning met

that most illustrious and charming actress, Mrs. D. P. Bowers, and was questioned by her in reference to this latest work.

After listening to a *résumé* of the piece, she made arrangements to have it read to her, saying she was " on the lookout for a new play, and so far this one seemed likely to interest her." Accordingly, the following day the reading took place, after which she discussed the work from beginning to end, expressing herself as thoroughly pleased, and complimenting the author in the highest terms. Finally, to bring the affair to a business basis, she said she had heard nothing so strong and so apparently fitted to make a success for her since she had starred " East Lynne ; " further stating that if Mr. A. M. Palmer would arrange to "send her out " with the necessary "backing " she would take the piece "on the road " without delay. All that had so far

transpired in relation to it was of sufficiently brilliant promise to make the
playwright feel convinced that the property now under consideration was liable
to realize a brilliant result at almost
any moment. A slight drop in the
barometer was experienced later, when
it was ascertained that Mrs. Bowers' efforts to obtain her "backing" had proved
futile ; theatrical business was not good
at the time, and Mr. Palmer did not
feel in condition to risk the necessary
funds.

Later on in the season when Miss
Wainwright and Mr. James came to
New York to fulfil their annual theatrical engagement, the product of their
suggestions was read to them, and both
pronounced it one of the strongest
pieces to which they had ever listened,
writing letters to the author to that
effect, and regretting at the same time
the fact of their being "billed" to play
in the "legitimate" only, thus prevent-

ing their presenting the play to the public themselves.

The playwright now decided to test the practical merits of the piece by giving it at a trial *matinée*, and with this purpose in view took it to Mr. H. B. Taylor, conducting "Taylor's Theatrical Exchange," desiring him to take charge of the business management of the affair, getting the "cast" together, etc.

Mr. Taylor was willing to undertake the matter, opining that the play would be a success, and "there would be money in it."

It was decided to hire the "Madison Square Theatre," then under the management of Mr. Palmer, for the representation; and as it was the rule that all plays produced at Mr. Palmer's theatre should pass under his scrutiny for several reasons, the chiefest among them being that he should find them fitting in all respects, it was taken to him for

perusal.   Within twenty-four hours
the playwright called for the play and
the verdict, to find that Mr. Palmer and
his "reader" had meantime made
themselves familiar with its contents
and were more than favorably disposed
towards it, Mr. Palmer's only objection
being that it seemed to him too strong
at that period for the taste of a public
that only seemed to be gratified by
farce-comedy and burlesque.   However,
this was only a suggestion of possible
taste, the arrangements for the *matinée*
were begun.   The first person engaged
for the company was Mr. Maurice Barrymore, to enact the leading male *rôle.*

Upon hearing the play read he was
enthusiastic in regard to it, and also
more than ordinarily interested by a
certain coincidence relating to it.   It
seems the French novel that had afford-
ed the author the nucleus of the plot
had at one period attracted his attention
also ; in fact, he had been so impressed

with its strong dramatic qualities that
he had himself essayed to found a play
upon it, but, according to his own account, had failed to be satisfied with the
result, and now that he had chanced
upon the same idea worked out to his
liking, he was more than willing to
undertake the designated *rôle*.

While the present phase in the fortunes of the play was pending, Mr.
Alexander Salvini walked into Mr.
Taylor's office one afternoon when the
latter was conducting a business interview with the author, and being in-
structed as to the subject, and thereby
becoming somewhat interested, it was
suggested he should read the play and
submit his opinion of it.

He took the MS. with him, and in
the course of a day or two returned with
it, saying that he was most favorably
impressed with the plot, its strength,
and so on, and believed it had every
chance of success. It was not in the

line of the plays in his *repertoire*, and, therefore, as there would be some risk for him in producing it, he would not like to undertake the entire responsibil- ity, but if the author would advance the funds for the first week's production, he would guarantee the second week, at the end of which time it could be deter- mined if the play would carry itself and be in for a "run."

The author, however, would not con- sent to this, for the piece having already received the *cachet* of so many dis- tinguished people in the profession, it seemed as though much better terms should be demanded for it.

The latter was apparently justified in these views, as within a day or two Mr. James Barton Key, upon hearing of the play and learning its plot, became posi- tively excited over it.

"Why," said he, "it is most remark- able that I should finally run across this piece. For six years past I have been

enthusiastic over the book that suggested it, and could not for the life of me
understand why some one did not recog-
nize its possibilities and make a play of
it. A trial *matinée!*" he ejaculated
to the author in a tone of disgust.
"No—you must not dream of it, the
piece is far too good to run the chance of
ruining it in any such fashion. It
must be properly produced for a 'run,'
and I'll undertake to do it."

Fired by Mr. Key's enthusiasm, the
author put a stop to all further prepara-
tions for a *matinée*, and entered into
work with him in dead earnest, to fulfil
their contemplated arrangements for a
production.

Mr. Barrymore was held for the leading *rôle* as before ; Mr. E. J. Henly engaged to personate the "polished vil-
lain," and the cast in general was an
exceptionally good one.

After the expenditure of much time
and energy, Mr. Key succeeded in find-

ing a man who was willing to "back" the enterprise, that is, guarantee the expenses for three weeks. The next step was to obtain a desirable theatre, an exceedingly difficult matter in New York, by the way, towards the end of a theatrical season.

None were found available until a consultation with Mr. Henry Miner revealed the fact that it might be possible to "book" time at the "Fifth Avenue," of which he had the management, if a certain "star," who had been vacillating in the matter, could be persuaded to cancel her engagement.

Under the circumstances, Mr. Key regarded the selection of a theatre as settled, and went on perfecting the rest of his arrangements.

Some very handsome scenery and furniture, in storage for debt, and that had been used in one of Mrs. Potter's plays, was secured ; in fact, everything seemed to "move on wheels." The messages exchanged between the "star" and the manager were eminently satisfactory until within a comparatively short period of the date set for the " opening night," when this "star," making use of the prerogative of her sex, suddenly upset the calculations of every one by telegraphing that she had decided after all to play her three weeks in New York.

There was no other theatre to be had, and by the time there would be one vacant the hot weather would be too far advanced to make the attempt feasible or practical.

The playwright and Mr. Key were obliged to stand this blow as best they could, and turn their attention and efforts elsewhere.

The latter subsequently sent an aspiring and handsome young actress, emanating from the west, to the author, with word that, should the play suit her, she would have unlimited money to spend

on its production. The play did suit
her, with the exception that she desired
the part of the heroine to be still further
emphasized if possible.

The author succeeded in accomplishing this, and greatly improving the
piece generally at the same time, but
when everything was again in readi-
ness, the affluent young actress had
become a poor young actress. Her
" backer " having vanished, and in place
of securing a permanency for herself
amidst the constellations, she was per-
force contented to take a third-rate
position in a " stock " company.

Upon the return of Mr. Louis James
to New York at the close of the season, he made haste to visit the author
to say that during these intervening
months, the play had so haunted him,
and he had become so convinced that it
was "a good thing," that he had about
decided to alter his policy, that is,
abandon the " legitimate " for the fol-

lowing season, and arrange to take the piece "out."

He took the MS. away with him, becoming more and more impressed with. it, pencilling out his scenes and the "business" in preparation for a production. No contracts had yet been signed, however, and meantime Mr. Morrissey had made several engagements with Miss Rose Coghlan to hear the play read. One circumstance after another arose to prevent this latter, and at last the minds of every one concerned were put at rest by Mr. James' assurance that the matter, as far as he was concerned, might be regarded as settled.

Such proved not to be the case, for the following day came a hurried note from the tragedian saying he regretted, as much as possibly the author would, not being able to produce the piece, his *rôle* in it being delightfully adapted to him, but that he had just received an

3

offer from Mr. Frederick Warde with
which he had closed, and their *répertoire*
would continue to embrace only the
" legitimate." One of the principal
reasons he assigned for the change was
that the responsibility of management
would thus be lifted off his hands. As
time went on, several of the lesser lights
read and approved the play, but never
found themselves in condition to raise
the necessary funds for production, and
during this lull, as it were, Mrs. Bowers
sent another request that the play should
be read to her, as she thought there was
once more some possibility of her obtaining a " backer ; " but for the second time
she failed in accomplishing this.

Miss Emily Rigl was the next " star "
on the *tapis* to become interested, but
the "backing," or rather the lack of it,
played its usual part of stumbling-block.

Personally Miss Rigl makes it a point
never to risk anything, and, at the time,
no one could be found who would risk

for her, so it went on to the next, who proved to be Mr. E. J. Henley. He having heard considerable of the piece, and having been engaged to act in it, though so far not having heard the play itself, went to see the author about it. At the same time he was busily engaged on a venture of his own, and therefore not in a position to give immediate attention to this one, but, if successful with the first, proposed to follow it up with a representation of the work referred to should it meet his demands.

He took the MS. away with him. Shortly after, the piece in which he was interested was produced, failed, and he was taken ill. In the general disturbance he of course failed to read the play the fortunes of which we are following, and finally sent it back to the owner (who was now becoming perfectly accustomed to this result), and left the city in search of health.

Mr. Jacob Litt, having heard of the

work, next took it up to read, but being almost simultaneously sent for to super- intend and disentangle some of the troubles occurring in his western thea- tres returned the play unread to the author, to be " considered further upon his return to New York."

One day the playwright read it to Miss Julia Arthur, and it seemed from the immediate result as though it had found its niche at last. She was charmed with it in every way, being enthusiastic over the *rôle* of the heroine, which would, she said, suit her better than any she had so far been entrusted to portray. Though under contract to Mr. A. M. Palmer as "leading lady" of his "stock" company, she decided to try and use her influence in getting him to stage it for her, thus giving her a decided opportunity for displaying her powers.

Mr. Palmer was about sailing for Europe, and was finally persuaded to take the revised MS. with him, to consider the feasibility meantime of producing the play the ensuing fall, with Miss Arthur in the title-rôle. When he returned to this country, it happened to be on the ship that was held in quarantine for twenty days down the bay during the cholera scare, and upon finally reaching the city he told Miss Arthur and the playwright, that, though greatly impressed with the strength of the play, and under the circumstances he should like to oblige them both, absolutely the policy of his theatre would not allow of his producing anything of so melodramatic an order. Up to date there are half a dozen people taking this same piece under consideration.

The author constantly threatens to let the manuscript go up in a semblance of a blaze of glory by touching a match to it, averring the fact of being sick and tired of the whole thing ; but upon the occasion of each threat of this nature a protest is uttered against the sacrifice, and a reminder that many of those that have turned out to be the so-called "great plays" have had just such a history. So the MS. still remains MS., and is still pigeon-holed, notwithstanding the fact that it has a dozen times been within an ace of production. Hope need not necessarily be crushed out, even by playwrights experiencing such vicissitudes as above recounted, when it is borne in mind that the immortal Gounod waited and watched through ten dreary years before his no less immortal opera of "Faust" received its production.

Louis James in Comedy.

ACCUSTOMED to seeing Louis James in tragic *rôles,* or at all events in the legitimate drama, the public is not aware that it has been deprived of a delightful comedian.

His ability in this line, as well as his wonderful command of an adverse situation, was perfectly displayed upon the occasion of a large "benefit performance" several years ago. Mr. James' contribution to the entertainment was to take the leading part in a one-act comedy from the French; the two other characters in the piece being impersonated by Miss Bruno, a handsome English blonde, and Mr. Burr McIntosh, just then beginning to appear on Metropolitan boards.

The rehearsals of that comedy were,

I am sure, infinitely more ludicrous than the author had ever anticipated. No especial place had been provided for the trio to rehearse in, and no one deputed to hold the prompt-book, so it resulted in a sort of " go-as-you-please " in a private drawing-room, and a closing with the modest offer of an amateur as prompter. Though excessively pains-taking, considerable verdancy was mani-fested by Miss Bruno, Mr. McIntosh and the stage-manager *pro tem.* The latter, unversed in the ways of the true " professional," frequently felt as if tied up in knots by Mr. James' methods of rehearsing, which seemed to consist of a mumbling and jumbling of words, the only part that was ever distinct being the cue.

The actor finally made the uneasy prompter, who was in a continuous rush to " find the place," understand that he never, if he could avoid it, repeated anything that took place in the play at

rehearsal, except the cue. After this
they got on fairly well together, although arriving at the desired period
by a series of spasmodic jumps. As for
Mr. McIntosh, he was usually immersed
in thought or studying his "part" at
the moment his cue was given, and
would tardily arrive upon the scene
displaying great surprise that it was
"his turn," or else, being over-warned,
would precipitate himself forward several speeches too soon. Nor was he as
well "up" in French as he is at present,
and would insist upon addressing Mr.
James in the play as " Octive, Octive,
old fellow," suggesting thereby a certain number of notes on the piano. The
prompter one day "walked in where
angels fear to tread," making Mr. Mc-
Intosh aware of his *bétise* by suggesting that he should sometimes pronounce
it Octave, as in the French, but was
incontinently snubbed by the young
man in return, who did not relish being

" taken up afore folks," observing
irritably, "Oh ! that'll be all right at
the performance." A quickly suppressed
glance of merriment appeared in Mr.
James' eyes during this little encounter,
and I am positive during the rehearsals
he experienced many delicious silent
paroxyms of mirth, his fine sense of the
ludicrous being amply fed by the un-
conscious food of his "support."

The day of the performance, strange
to say, from such unpromising premises,
proved a veritable triumph for James.
Before his " Public " he bent to the
serious task before him—serious, because
at the rise of the curtain the members
of his small cast became what is known
in the vernacular as " rattled." They
walked " On " and " Off " whenever
impelled, said anything that came into
their minds at the time, and if nothing
came Mr. James smilingly supplied the
defect with an impromptu. McIntosh
sailed around calling upon " Octive " to

his heart's content, and the amateur prompter sat in the stage-box aghast, recognizing hardly any of the original piece being given to the audience.

The apparently rudderless bark proved to be in more than safe hands, however, and came to its moorings miraculously. As he afterwards explained, Mr. James very soon perceived that his "support," vulgarly speaking, was not "in it," and so coined everything necessary on the spot, succeeding thereby in producing a comedy "while you wait" that kept the large audience in a continuous roar of laughter, and covered himself with glory. In speaking of the affair he said he never enjoyed anything better in his life—and I'll venture to say the audience rendered the same verdict.

The Tragedian and the Rubber Band.

In pursuance of the humorous side of Mr. Louis James' character, several incidents occur to me connected with his public and private life which happened to come within my knowledge.

Possibly somewhat in sympathy with Silas Wegg, he frequently " falls into poetry," in his private correspondence; but as it is highly probable he would not allow these hasty effusions to be dignified by this much-abused term, I hasten to do justice to that innate modesty which is another characteristic of Mr. James, and simply designate them as verses. A short prose preface is necessary, however, before submitting the lines I have in mind.

Upon a certain occasion the actor surprised and delighted a young friend

of his who had just concluded her
" maiden effort " at play-writing by expressing sincere admiration for the result, and assuring her if, upon closer
consideration, the piece confirmed the
impression obtained from it upon the
first reading, he would probably produce
it during his coming " season."

"Ah !" said he, laying the MS.
open at a page that seemed to have
caught his eye, and evidently at the same
time experiencing some difficulty in
keeping his features under grave control, " here is one of your stage directions I shall hardly be able to comply
with."

" What is that ?" demanded the anxious young author.

" This one," replied Mr. James, reading : " ' *L. D. enters slowly B. C.*"
" Now I can't do that, you know,"
said he, glancing up from the page with
a very ingenuous expression of countenance.

"But why not?" asked the puzzled young woman.

"Because," replied Mr. James with mock gravity, "though '*L. D.*' may have found it convenient to come in at that period, Louis James, his representative to be, is, unfortunately, an A. D.'er, and is therefore obliged to enter 'up to date.'" He thereupon indulged in a hearty laugh at the expense of the little playwright, assuring her, however, it was but a slight mistake easily remedied, and proceeded to illustrate that the C., minus the B., would prove an all-sufficient guide to the ordinarily intelligent Thespian, though, in further conversations, he could not always restrain himself from making some playful allusion to the time when she insisted that "he should enter before Christ."

At the time referred to, it was finally arranged that the MS. should be sent to Mr. James' hotel the following day, and in tying up the package the author, for further safety, slipped a rubber band around it, somewhat over an inch wide. In an accompanying note she suggested the band was but a loan, being a valuable piece of property, which she should expect to have returned with the MS. ; further insinuating he should keep watch and ward of his conscience in the matter, lest it should serve for some odious comparison 'twixt it and the elastic.

The mail very shortly brought an acknowledgment of the MS., the following short extract from the note serving to show the impression created by the unusual size of the rubber :

" CHERIE ELASTIC :
   " *Where* did you get it, and by what means?
   " Have you a corner on rubber?
   " I accept the 'trust,' but deny the similarity between it and my conscience, etc., etc.
      " Signed,
         " Yours in the Lord,
            " LOUISA,
            "Exit B. C."

Meantime a theatrical manager sent in haste to the young lady for the MS. of this same play, saying he desired to read it to Miss Rose Coghlan. Somewhat elated with her sudden popularity in the "stellar" world, the young authoress sent a hasty request to Mr. James for the return of her play for a day or two. The messenger brought it back almost immediately, without any accompanying word from him, and minus—the rubber band.

Fearing in her haste to have offended Mr. James, she subsequently wrote him an explanatory note, and added a playful request for the missing rubber.

It came next day by express, done up in numberless wrappings and a cardboard box.

Her sex being allowed a "change of mind," the young lady generously decided to present the much-worried rubber to Mr. James out and out. Accordingly, in preparation, she placed

LOUIS JAMES in "Virginius."

the band on a piece of gilded cardboard, fastening it in place at intervals with pale blue ribbon in the form of "true lovers' knots," and inscribing within the circle these lines :

TO

LOUIS JAMES.

" Tho' you have won the '*rubber*' in this game,
  I cherish no ill-feeling for the same.
  These true-blue knots at intervals of space,
  To keep my too elastic love in place."

M.

Mr. James, evidently considering the game was not yet "played out," forwarded the following within twenty-four hours :

"SWEET MAID,

" Your love ' elastic,' can it be?
  I've always found you trusting true,
  That's the way you've *been* to me ;
  Ye gods ! Now, what am I to do?

"If you, like this band of rubber,
  Hold on *all* the things you meet,
  How I wish I was your ' lubber,'
  To be held by one so sweet.

4

" But rubber comes, and rubber goes,
  Sometimes one way, sometimes t'other ;
  Comes in *garters*, comes in *hose;*
  If you doubt me, ask your mother.

" Oh, you giddy, heartless critter,
  Draped in clinging things, and lace,
  Don't your conscience *sometimes* twitter,
  When you see my careworn face ?

" Now, adieu ; don't think me bold
  (I'm sitting in my *robe de nuit*) ;
  And I know I'm catching cold
  While inditing this to thee.

" Thus, when as marble cold I lay,
  With a *Daisy* in my hand,
  Surely friends will truly say,
  Died of too much ' Rubber Band.'

                    " *Exit* ' LOUISA.'
                    " ' A '(*n*) ' D '(*ante*)."

The *woman*, in the recipient of the above, not feeling content to allow a man, even though a distinguished actor, the privilege of the "last word," decided to send Mr. James a line of sympathy on his decease, and at the same time give the matter in general a decent burial, the means being appropriately at hand in the form of an envelope, and paper to match, about ten inches by

six in size, the whole bordered by a
solid inch of black, the style used by the
French when in mourning, for conveying to friends the news of a death.

At the top of the sheet of paper the
young authoress drew a good-sized pair
of scissors, these to serve as her right-
ful crest. Finding a bunch of black
flowers in a newspaper, she pasted them
on one of the lower corners of the same
page, and wrote on the clear space left :

IN MEMORIAM.

" Not a voice was heard, not an eye was dry,
  Through the width and breadth of the land,
  As they gravely closed the coffin lid
  On—the tune from the Rubber Band."

A little black cat, illustrating one
of the advertisements of a periodical,
served, when cut out, to fasten the flap
of the envelope, accompanied by the
Latin, arranged for the occasion,

" REQUIES

S'CAT

IN SPACE "—

It was then directed—

"To the deceased,"
Louis James
—— Theatre,

with a note in one corner—

"If in communication, please forward."

The appearance of such a document in the post must undoubtedly have produced a startling effect upon those through whose hands it passed, before reaching its destination.

The following day, Mr. James called upon the fair playwright, to talk over the matter of the play, as well as to comment on the above. She appeared, attired in a long white gown, to the left shoulder of which was attached an immense black gauze bow; she wore long black gloves, and carried a black fan, her features drawn to a "decent gravity."

She of course anticipated that with Mr. James' usual keenness he would immediately connect her costume with the elastic incident. To her surprise, however, he came quickly forward to meet her, and in a voice of deep concern anxiously inquired what had happened so suddenly, "Had any of the family——?"

With a delighted laugh at having caught the tragedian "napping," she explained that she was only evincing a proper respect for the demise of—the "Rubber Band."

Characteristic of Maurice Barrymore.

THE difficulties encountered and the length of time it takes in communicating with distinguished members of the theatrical profession may be well illustrated in the person of Mr. Maurice Barrymore, and after perusing the following it will be easily comprehended why he, at all events, would be accessible to but few.

A playwright, desiring to produce a play at a matinée "on trial," concluded Barrymore was the most desirable man for the leading *rôle*, and accordingly deputed an agent to make an appointment with him.

The writer, having had no previous personal experience with Mr. Barrymore, prepared to meet the actor within a few days, but, despite the earnest en-

deavors of the agent, a theatrical manager and several friends, who tried to
deliver messages, six months elapsed
before the desired interview took place.

When it did, the playwright felt assured it was as difficult, once located, for
the actor to go as it had been to come.

It happened to be a bitter cold day in
winter, and when, after three or four
hours of reading and discussion, Mr.
Barrymore rose, carelessly observing,
"Well, I think I'll be going; I left a
friend of mine outside, Gus Thomas,
who walked over with me"—and with
a slight smile adding, "I told him I
should only stop a moment," the playwright, quite horrified, exclaimed,
"Why, the poor fellow must be quite
frozen!"

"Oh, no, I fancy not," lazily observed
Barrymore; "and, by the way, I had a
terrible scene with him last night." As
he spoke the actor reseated himself.
"Thomas has got a play he wants me

to 'star' in, 'Reckless Temple' by name, and I'm averse to starring at present, but he stayed with me nearly all night, urging that this would afford him his one chance of becoming known in the world," etc., etc.

Mr. Barrymore remained fully another half-hour recounting the existing condition of affairs, and, despite the playwright's anxiety, it was made evident later on that Mr. Thomas did not freeze, and the good heart of the actor manifested itself as well, for " Reckless Temple" made its appearance on the "boards," with Mr. Barrymore in the title-*rôle*.

Though ultimately a failure, the piece apparently proved the stepping-stone he anticipated for Mr. Thomas, who has been known to fame and prosperity ever since, although Mr. Barrymore, upon the occasion referred to, certainly gave him, as he had others, a "long wait."

A Dispute Preceding the Professional Debut of Mrs. James Brown Potter.

THE fever termed "stage fever" is one from which those who have every reason for remaining in private life, such as position, means and family ties, should jealously guard themselves against. It is an insidious malady and, unless in the case of pronounced genius or the necessity for earning a living, should be stamped out as vigorously as any other plague.

I do not say this from any ill-feeling, being a sincere admirer of the stage in all its legitimate bearings, but because of a rooted objection to seeing women possessed of no real talent, break up their homes to make guys of themselves, and misery for their relatives and

friends.   Private theatricals seem to be
the " hot-bed " for instilling hope in the
aspirant for stage honors ; members of
these clubs would not for the world be
thought anything but " amateurs,"
and equally of course, "We only do it
for charity and the fun of the thing,"
is the invariable reply to any one who
utters a warning word, but gradually
one person will display some slight
talent, and his or her vanity is instantly
fed to repletion by the fulsome praise of
ill-advised friends.   That person becomes
the " star " of the club, and visions of
Sara Bernhardt and Henry Irving grow
dim, as the feeling within them becomes
a certainty that, "given the opportunity," and he or she will eclipse them all.

As an example of the foregoing, I
don't think a better choice occurs to me
than Mrs. James Brown Potter.   She
was an undoubted social favorite, commanding the admiration of her husband,
friends and acquaintances, so that when-

ever she made her appearance on the
amateur stage backed by the laudable
purpose of so doing for sweet charity's
sake, she was sure of an enthusiastic
audience. She became the recipient of
flattery more untrammelled than that
usually accorded an acknowledged
public favorite, and because of her
beauty and prestige was accorded the
place of society's leading amateur.

About this time, feeling that she was
getting quite beyond the casual one-day
or night performances given at intervals
during a "season," the organization of
which she was the leading light extended its operations accordingly, and
would play two or three successive
nights in the theatres of the small
cities adjacent to New York, always of
course—" for charity."

A faint whisper finally rippled through
Mrs. Potter's "set," to the effect that
she was seriously contemplating the
step that would designate her as a " pro-

fessional ; " rumor added that she was
receiving fabulous offers from would-
be managers, but when one bolder than
the others inquired the truth of Mrs.
Potter, the rumors were always denied.

Notwithstanding her denials, Mrs.
Potter, knowing Mrs. John Sherwood to
be intimate at the house of Mrs. Lester
Wallack, succeeded through her in
arranging an interview at which Mr.
Wallack should be present and hear her
recite, presumably with the idea of obtaining his estimate of her capabilities
as an actress.   At the close of her recitations, Mr. Wallack paid Mrs. Potter
several graceful compliments upon her
" charming talent," etc., such as he
deemed so pretty a woman as she had
a right to expect from him, but at the
same time very strongly advised her
not to become " professional," for, as he
observed after her departure, the moder-
ate amount of capacity she displayed
did not warrant her in throwing off her

responsibilities and breaking up her home, or him in offering such advice.

A little later on, a large benefit performance in aid of some good work was organized by one of the prominent women in society. It was to take place at the "Academy of Music," and for it the very best theatrical talent had volunteered their services. There were five hundred well-known women's names on the list of patronesses and, to represent these, Mrs. Potter was asked to read a very pretty prologue, written for the occasion by Mrs. John Sherwood.

Mrs. Potter returned a note of thanks and acceptance to the lady in charge of the affair, saying she would be happy to read the *prologue*, "before or after the performance."

The little difficulty in reference to appropriate time suggested by Mrs. Potter's note was easily adjusted, as she received a response from the busy man-

ageress *pro tem.*, saying she thought
they would not deviate from the prevailing custom upon this occasion, therefore she would like to have Mrs. Potter
open the performance with the prologue.

The project grew and prospered, was
much talked of, and, as the important
day drew near, was widely advertised.

Posters appeared on the elevated rail-
road stations, bearing, besides the announcement of the mammoth entertainment, the names of the prominent patronesses, and a list of those who had
volunteered to take part.

The placing of Mrs. Potter's name
proved a difficulty. As a large proportion of the volunteers were "stars" of
the first theatrical magnitude, it was
not deemed correct to head the list
with an amateur, even though it were
Mrs. James Brown Potter ; accordingly
it was placed about third on the list of
women's names. As it happened, in
the male list the name of Kyrle Bellew

appeared almost opposite that of Mrs. Potter, quite an accident of course, as I believe at that time they had barely met.

It being now very close to the date determined upon for the performance, the house of the manageress presented a very busy scene, the various people connected with the entertainment constantly coming and going; and among the visitors on a particular morning was Mrs. Potter, who had come to gain a few particulars as to the hour she was expected to appear, etc., etc. One of the posters previously mentioned happened to be spread out on a table in the drawing-room, and Mrs. Potter, attracted by her own name, stopped involuntarily and exclaimed, " Oh ! I am afraid Mr. Potter will not approve of that."

" Why should he object ?" inquired the lady. " All of our names are there as well, and the object is certainly a worthy one." Mrs. Potter, however, did not seem to feel at ease so far as Mr. Potter was concerned, and did not believe he would take kindly to her "professional" surroundings.

Her hostess then good-naturedly remarked, though she had not at present very much spare time at her disposal for arranging differences, if Mrs. Potter found her husband had any serious feeling.on the subject, to ask him to come and see her, and she would endeavor to explain the matter to his satisfaction.

That afternoon Mr. and Mrs. Potter called upon the lady in question, and, though a number of persons were present besides, the interview reached the storm boundary. Mr. Potter's anger was not of the repressed order, in fact he was loud and eloquent upon the subject of his wife's name being placed with those of "professionals," and gradually, from the drift of his words, it dawned upon his listeners that he had been given to understand that the entertainment was only to include the services of amateurs, and his first intimation that such was not the case came to him upon seeing the bill-boards referred to, at the elevated road stations.

From this aspect of affairs he was of course entitled to consideration, and although up to this moment the hostess was feeling herself somewhat aggrieved, knowing as she did that Mrs. Potter was fully cognizant of the arrangementsas they stood, as this new light was shed, she grasped the true situation, and when Mr. Potter's arrival at a period offered her the opportunity, she said, "You surely did not consider me so lacking in intelligence, Mr. Potter, as to hire the 'Academy of Music' for an *amateur* performance?"

Darting a look at his wife, Mr. Potter admitted it had appeared a strange arrangement to him, and then, as though his feelings upon the subject could no longer be held in check, he told Mrs,

5

Potter, in unmistakable language, that "this sort of thing had got to stop," she must be "black or white, an actress or not an actress." That these various affairs in which she took part that were in every essential "professional," and only prevented from so appearing to the public by the saving clause of "amateur" being tacked on, would no longer be tolerated. One of the most flagrant items, as regarded by Mr. Potter in the present instance, seemed to be the proximity of Kyrle Bellew's name to that of his wife, and causing him to remark he "simply wouldn't stand it."

In the latter part of the discourse Mrs. Potter seemed faintly to agree with her husband, though this may have been an undiscriminating acquiescence offered with the laudable intention of soothing him into an ordinary frame of mind ; to those present at the interview, however, who remembered and contrasted it by the light of after events, it seemed as though Mr. Potter must have felt some prophetic warning at the time.

The Potters finally arose to take their leave, Mr. Potter intimating that he should probably withdraw his wife's name from the programme, his wife at the same time assuring one of the ladies near her, *sotto voce*, that she should still hope to carry out her part, and would make every effort to alter her husband's ideas on the subject.

The result was Mrs. Potter's actual withdrawal by her husband, and Miss Marie Wainwright's more than gracious acceptance to take her place at the last moment, the press scenting out the whole affair, and interviews more or less true purporting to come from the warring factions appearing in the morning papers.

The *final* result of that interview, however, was made apparent a few months later, when the city was literally "painted red" with the announcement of the professional *début* of—Mrs. James Brown Potter, with the name of Mr. Kyrle Bellew in conjunction as her "leading man."

These so completely dwarfed the offending little elevated road posters, that I doubt if half a dozen persons remembered the acorn from which the great oak sprang.

Annoyances Attending a Theatrical Benefit Performance.

THE annoyances attendant upon the giving of a theatrical benefit performance are almost incalculable, more especially if the person in charge happens not to belong to the rank and file or managerial divisions of the profession. Their "good intentions" towards these then seems to count for naught, and the mere fact of being a "rank outsider" sufficient cause to create a suspicion and malice that leaves the trespasser on strange land a "hard row to hoe."

As an instance, I will detail the miseries experienced in the workings of one of these affairs by a young playwright.

Upon previous occasions, this enthusi-

astic young person had headed several
private enterprises which were so successful that from the proceeds of the
same she had had the pleasure of sending in many hundreds of dollars to the
"Actors' Fund." This was a pet charity with her, for the players themselves,
she argued, having given her so much
pleasure and entertainment all her life
in witnessing their performances, it
was but a fair return to think somewhat of their needs, and alleviate them
when possible. So that at the time of
the great Actors' Fund Fair, held at the
Madison Square Garden, in April, 1892,
her services were not to be overlooked,
and at the request of the Fund's President, Mr. A. M. Palmer, she consented
to organize a "benefit" to be given at
his theatre the week the Fair was being
held in the "Garden."

She had but a few weeks in which to
accomplish her work, and had at first
objected to the undertaking on the plea

of not having just the material at hand she desired, giving Mr. Palmer to understand that the following would be the best she could accomplish at the time, viz.: Put the finishing touches to two one-act plays of her own, a tragedy and comedy respectively, and, between these plays, a programme could be arranged consisting of music, recitations and dancing. If this bill should be considered sufficiently attractive, she would proceed; if not, she would be obliged to withdraw. The plays were submitted to Mr. Palmer to read, and his approval of the programme in general was signified by his placing his theatre and all comprised therein at the lady's disposal. He referred her to the late and deeply lamented Mr. Chas. W. Thomas, then Secretary for the "Fund," and co-manager and partner with Mr. Chas. Hoyt of the "Madison Square Theatre," for whatever information or assistance she would require (Mr.

Palmer being too deeply engaged with the Fair to be available for aught else), also naming his stage-manager, Mr. Gene W. Presbrey, as being at her service in directing rehearsals and to act as general stage-manager of the performance.

Matters so arranged presented a very roseate hue at the outset, and the young author, having finished her plays, turned her attention to the executive branch of the entertainment.

The first thing, of course, was to secure the two volunteer casts required, and this Mr. Thomas and Mr. Presbrey said that between them they would accomplish, although the playwright found her services were quite frequently· required.

This or that actor or actress could not or would not accept for divers reasons all-sufficient to themselves, for, be it known, let me remark *en passant*, the profession (for which I cannot blame them) are not all too fond of studying and dressing a part for a single performance, even though it be for charity, and that charity their own.

Finally, however, the cast for the tragedy was complete, Mr. Louis James, Mr. Edward Bell and Miss Julia Arthur in the leading *rôles*, the maller parts being filled by members of Mr. Palmer's "stock" company, so rehearsals forthis piece were immediately called.

Mr. Presbrey thought there would be no difficulty in casting the comedy, as Mr. Daniel Frohman, or other managers of comedy companies, would willingly loan a sufficient number of their people, and feeling satisfied the plays were now in good hands, the young playwright turned her attention to the speciality portion of the programme.

There were many difficulties to be encountered here : good artists, especially among the musicians, had not finished their "season" and were still "on the road," more particularly the opera comique contingent, including Miss Lillian Russell, Miss Marie Tempest, Carl Streetman, Hubert Wilke and others. She wrote to many of these, upon the chance that they would return to New York in time, requesting their services, but their replies were for the most part discouraging.

After great patience and a lavish use of note-paper, she obtained the acceptance of Sig. Campanini to sing.

"Red tape" with singers appears to be indispensable ; they are so proverbially independent, and will sometimes do for a caprice what a large sum of money would not force from them.

Sig. Campanini's services were first requested in the name of the "Actors' Fund." He refused. Then in the name of Mr. and Mrs. Palmer ; but, for reasons best known to himself, he would not sing for anything or any-

body other than at the simple request
of the young amateur manageress.

Conditions, by this time, had become
as nothing to her : she accepted all and
every kind, keeping in view only the
results. An interruption occurred here
in this branch of her labors—the or-
ganist required to play the organ at a
certain point of the tragedy was called
for ; she immediately made heroic
efforts in the organists' ranks to obtain
a good volunteer, but met with no success, until, going into the Mason &
Hamlin ware-rooms one morning, she
was offered the services of Mr. Wm. C.
Carl, who had just returned, with his
laurel wreaths, from Paris, as well as
the promise of a very fine instrument
to be used at the *matinée.*

After further efforts, the late Mme.
Schirener-Mapleson, together with Miss
Rosa Linde, Miss Helen Von Doenhoff
and Sig. Clemento Bologna, were secured to complete the musical numbers.

Mr. Aubrey Boucicault, in a gracious way truly grateful to the now much worried manageress, consented to recite, and Omijo San and Oyaye San, Japanese dancers from the Imperial Court of Japan, were allowed by their managers to give a characteristic national dance.

One of the women having charge of a booth at the Fair was instrumental in obtaining the latter attraction, and, in return for this, illustrated the intense desire of which many people are possessed for obtaining free passes to a theatre.

She called at Mr. Thomas' office in the " Madison Square Theatre " building to offer the services of the dancers, the young playwright happening to enter at the same time. The former, having transacted her business, turned to the latter, saying : "I should like to have you send me a couple of complimentary tickets for the performance, so that I may come for the short time I can leave my booth at the Fair and see these girls dance."

The playwright quietly reminded her that the entertainment was being given for *charity*, and consequently "complimentaries" could not be distributed.

The woman continued to urge the matter as her right, until Mr. Thomas assured her that what she asked was impossible. Upon hearing this she literally "flounced" out of the office.

"Is she poor?" inquired the young lady.

"Poor!" ejaculated Mr. Thomas. "Come and look at her carriage."

The former, approaching the window, saw the woman drive away in a handsome equipage, coachman and footman occupying the box.

It was within ten days of the performance when the playwright, upon going to "Palmer's Theatre" one morning, received word that Mr. Presbrey would like to speak to her.

Entering his private office, she was both astonished and displeased to have him tell her, after some preamble, though he regretted hurting her feelings, he should really advise her to give up the proposed "benefit."

After an instant's hesitation, she merely reminded Mr. Presbrey he was scarcely in a position to "hurt her feelings," but bade him offer his reasons for the foregoing.

He thereupon intimated that the real trouble consisted in the immoral tone of the tragedy, and, in consequence, Miss Arthur had that morning thrown down her book at rehearsal and refused to goon.

"And what else?" inquired his listener.

Well, Mr. Frohman would not be able to loan them his people for the comedy; in fact, here was his letter upon the subject. A typewritten sheet was handed to her, signed by Daniel Froh-

man. The gist contained therein was to
the effect that Mr. Frohman regretted
that he should need his people for the
rehearsal of a new piece. Glancing up
from the page, she remarked to the
stage-manager, that all this was of course
very annoying, but the affair being
advertised, it was naturally too late
to turn back, therefore, the only thing to
be done was to re-cast the plays as
quickly as possible.

The stage-manager, without replying
directly, attempted to give the young
lady some advice as to re-writing her
play, at the same time persisting that it
would be impossible to go on with the
arrangements for the "benefit."

The lady then very plainly assured
him that, at Mr. Palmer's request, she
had already put herself to a great deal
of trouble in getting up this affair, which
was none of her own seeking, that her
play was not even suggested as being
immoral either by him or other leading

people, that she had no intention of re-writing it, and, as stage-manager under existing circumstances, his opinion upon the subject was not required.

Finally, that, in any event, the " benefit " would take place, and all she desired from him at present was Miss Arthur's address. This she had great difficulty in obtaining, being assured it was absolutely of no use for her to see the actress, but the playwright being de-termined, and the stage-manager hav-ing no good reason for withholding the same, it was finally put in her posses-sion.

Calling first to see Mr. Thomas, the young lady discovered he had already heard rumors of dissension, and was thereby annoyed. She recounted to him the foregoing experience, and upon mentioning the letter she had seen from Mr. Frohman, Mr. Thomas wheeled round to his desk, and picking up a sheet of paper, handed it to her, remark-

ing, "This, then, must be the first half
of the same letter, sent me by Presbrey
this morning."

It was easy to surmise from this portion that the stage-manager had given
Mr. Frohman to understand that the
"benefit" was in reality a vehicle by
which the playwright intended exploit-
ing two of her plays, and, impressed
with this idea, Mr. Frohman declined to
give her the aid of his people.

Upon comprehending the situation
Mr. Thomas and the young author were
exceeding wroth. Mr. Thomas said he
had never known Dan Frohman to break
faith with him before, and up to the
present moment had been speculating
as to the cause. The stage-manager's
evident intention to break up the "benefit" he could not comprehend, unless
from the mere fact that he desired to
shirk the trouble it entailed ; their
mutual decision, at all events, was to
"repair damages" without loss of time,

6

the playwright's first move being to call upon Miss Arthur and learn the cause of her defection.

She found Miss Arthur rather impregnable at first, and evidently smothering some of the indignation that had not fully found vent; but the truth was out finally, and the actress's only reason for relinquishing her part appeared to be Mr. Presbrey's resolve, given out that morning at rehearsal, to "cut" certain portions of the play, until, as Miss Arthur declared, the process would eliminate all the strength and force from her *rôle*. Under the circumstances she declined to go on.

It was now the author's turn to become indignant once more.

"Then it was not what was in the play," she questioned, "but the threat of cutting some of it out that forced your decision?"

Receiving Miss Arthur's assent to this, she continued: "What right could the stage-manager have, under existing circumstances, to 'cut' or add anything to my play without consulting me ?"

" None whatever," rejoined Miss Arthur.

The actress then gave her promise to appear at "Palmer's Theatre" for rehearsal the following morning at ten o'clock, and, much relieved in mind, the young lady drove to the hotel where both Mr. James and Mr. Presbrey resided with their families.

Sending up her cards, she requested both gentlemen to meet her in the ladies' reception-room.

Mr. James made his appearance first, and rapidly laying the facts before him, she begged that he would go on with his "part," and also take the stage-management of the piece. Mr. James very kindly accepted both propositions, and when Mr. Presbrey entered the room, the young lady suggested that he

would be pleased to learn she had succeeded in every way ; that the original
cast would assemble at the theatre the
next morning for rehearsal, and at the
same time she would not require his
services, as Mr. James had consented to
act as stage-manager for the tragedy,
the comedy being now in the hands of
Mr. Thomas.

Mr. Presbrey endeavored to appear
as pleased at this announcement as the
playwright, and Mr. James felt inward-
ly convinced he was not, and complimented the former upon having sur-
mounted all difficulties.

There was some skirmishing along
the comedy line, but five days before
the date fixed for the *matinée*, the cast
was filled out by members of the " Trip
to Chinatown " company, and included
Queenie Vassar, Anna Boyd, Geraldine
McCann, Loie Fuller, Adolph Jack-
son, Ralph Bartlett and James K.
Hackett.

Under the able guidance of that most responsible of stage-managers, Mr. R. A. Roberts, the piece was brought up to an amazing state of perfection, considering there were less than half a dozen rehearsals.

Among the minor annoyances that continued were such as the following. The young lady could find no one who would take it upon themselves to keep the affair advertised, thus she was obliged to " work " that department to the best of her ability unaided. Again, stopping at the box-office of the theatre one. morning, she learned that the sale of seats had been suspended. Upon inquiring the cause of this disastrous move, she was told Mr. Palmer had been given to understand by his stage-manager that the "benefit" would not "come off," hence this order. After a little energy expended on her part "by word of mouth," this was rectified, and the sale continued.

The day of the performance arrived, and going to the theatre a little early to see that everything was in order, she found that the Mason & Hamlin organ just arrived at the scene entrance was being refused admission on account of its size ; the employees of the theatre assuring her the instrument was too large to be brought into the building. As the door for scenery happened to be two stories high, and the organ could have been placed in any room of ordinary height ceiling, the assertion was ridiculous on its face to any one present.

However, the young playwright, deciding that this was but one more annoyance she was being subjected to, wasted no words, but repaired to the organ ware-rooms, and selecting a smaller instrument, had it immediately sent to the theatre.

In view of the worries and difficulties she had been forced to undergo, it seemed almost a miracle that the benefit was conducted to the finish with complete success, and, according to the vernacular, there was "not a hitch" in the programme.

The companies of both pieces played as smoothly as though giving regular performances.

Campanini, as the paper stated later, sang better than he had in years, "creating one of his old-time *furores*," and the remaining numbers of music, recitation, etc., were rendered with a spirit that made those present, including members of the press, vote the afternoon a complete triumph.

You may rest assured the young author, who was largely responsible for this agreeable result, did not feel she had reached her goal on a bed of roses.

Reminiscent of the Vokes Family.

IT is possibly completing a round dozen of years since that delightful little theatrical company styled the " Vokes Family " gave their last performances in this country.

I only appeal to the " oldest inhabitants " to carry their memories back so far, but they, I am sure, will always retain pleasant thoughts of the clean, mirth-provoking entertainment with which these players furnished the public.

At the time of which I speak, (probably 1882), I was one of a large party summering at the " Ft. Wm. Henry " Hotel, Lake George, where the Vokes also arrived, bag and baggage, for a month's outing ; it was there that some of us had the pleasure of knowing them more or less well in their private life.

Rosina Vokes (the late Mrs. Cecil

Clay) remaining in England, her place in the "Family" was taken by Miss Bessie Sanson (now Mrs. Frank Daniels); otherwise the organization was the same, I am told, as when it made its first appearance in this country in "The Belles of the Kitchen."

Never were there three more respected and self-respecting young women on the boards than the Vokes sisters ; they were always as rigidly chaperoned by an aunt or their mother as any well-brought-up girls in society.

Late suppers, or visitors other than those who would call generally upon any family, were entirely debarred.

The aunt to whom I refer travelled with them for many years, wrote their plays, and always "had supper ready for her girls in their own rooms after the performance."

Fred Vokes, their brother (for Fawdon was only adopted), designed the scenery and arranged the music for their plays,

while between them they settled the
costuming. Thus, in all ways, the term
" Family," fittingly described them.

When at leisure from theatrical
duties, the girls were always sitting
together, engaged upon some piece of
that everlasting fancy-work so dear to
the heart of the Englishwoman.

The first appearance of the "Family"
at the "Ft. Wm. Henry" made a visible
impression ; it was at breakfast, and I
may say they were nothing if not independent in their dressing.

Victoria, Jessie and Miss Sanson were
attired in Watteau wrappers of different
hues, their aunt clad in black, with one
of those structures termed caps sur-
mounting her decorous, smooth brown
"front," composed of many yards of
black lace and ribbon, "relieved " by
bunches of violets. The men, of whom
there were four in the party, wore the
usual English summer morning *negligé*
costumes.

The entire party seemed utterly oblivious to the world surrounding them, and went their various ways in a perfectly frank, unaffected manner.

Those in the hotel whose lives heretofore had never happened to bring them in contact with members of the theatrical profession, at first rather resented their presence and were inclined to sit at a distance and regard them in the light of a menagerie " let loose ; " but as they did not evince the slightest desire to encroach on the territory or society of the *habitués* of the hotel, in fact, if anything, rather avoided it, a few days saw the former making advances to " the enemy " which, though not repulsed, were received without enthusiasm.   By the end of the first week, however, they were established favorites, adding greatly to the general gaiety, in their bright agreeable fashion.

In return for hospitalities they had

received from various guests of the hotel, they gave a picnic one day, to which quite a number of us were invited, and, I may add, there were no regrets.

They chose Diamond Island, a charming spot three miles up the lake from the " Ft. Wm. Henry," for the " happy hunting-ground," and I am sure I am correct in saying that no more delightful affair of its kind has ever been given in that region of repose and pleasure.

The means of transportation consisted of a fleet of row-boats, and, though the picnic lasted throughout the day, there was not a dull moment experienced. The details for the "spread" were perfect, the actual work of which was left in the hands of the English valets, the one exception to this being a chowder concocted by Fred Vokes, for which he was, and deserved to be, well complimented.

By the aid of the various musical instruments upon which the "Family" could perform, the air was frequently filled with delightful melody, and as the sun began its sinking journey back of the "purple hills," warning the pleasure-seekers to find shelter from the night, there were nothing but expressions of regret that "the day was done." Boat after boat was filled and launched out onto the glassy lake, and only the steady plash of the oars, and Fred Vokes' voice, as he sang a charming solo, disturbed the silent twilight.

Fred was possibly the most talented member of his family, being not only excessively clever in his nominal calling, but an artist in oils of no mean pretensions, a fine pianist, possessed of a good voice and innumerable minor accomplishments, but, as is often the case with genius, he was a great care, in this instance, to his sisters.

Generous and extravagant to a fault, he would hand out the last cent in his pocket to any one who asked for it, and was, in consequence, easy prey for the large army of impecunious actors who are always hanging about their successful brethren ; in his nature, a veritable Bohemian tramp.

At the lake he would don the most disreputable looking old garments, and sally forth, pipe in mouth, his fishing-rod and painting materials in hand. When he would next "turn up," was ofttimes a problem to the family ; frequently, it would be far into the night.

The last day of their stay at the "Ft. Wm. Henry," Fred was entreated not to leave the grounds, as they would be starting for Saratoga directly after the two o'clock dinner ; the sisters realizing from experience it was best if possible to keep their brother in sight. He faithfully promised to make his appearance in due time, and with this assurance went off as usual to muse on sea and sky.

The hours slipped away, dinner was over and the stage before the door. No Fred in sight. The baggage was being piled up mountain high, and the sisters were anxiously peering in every direction for the missing member, but not the smallest cloud of dust in the distance betokened his approach. Finally, the last bags and bundles being in place, they were obliged to take their seats on the coach and leave him to his fate.

As the driver cracked his whip preparatory to the start, Fred appeared, toiling up the hill from the lake, extremely warm in appearance, and tugging his rod and painting paraphernalia. Every one shouted to him "to hurry," to which admonition he paid but slight heed, and when he came within speaking distance, his sister Jessie, in horrified accents, exclaimed—
"You're never going to disgrace us by going to Saratoga in *that* 'get-up,' are you, Fred?"

For all answer Fred packed away his
traps on the coach, and, swinging himself up on one of the trunks strapped on
the back, which left his feet dangling in
nonchalant fashion, waved a good-bye
with his ragged hat to those on the
piazza, who could not help laughing at
the comical look of resignation that
overspread the faces of the feminine
portion of the party.

The last time I saw the Vokes was
one evening in the ensuing winter,
when, upon receiving a box with their
compliments, a party of us went to a
Brooklyn theatre where they were
playing "Fun in a Fog."

Of course the "Family" made all
sorts of covert allusions, for our benefit,
to their life at Lake George, not comprehended by the general audience :
but Fred finally outstripped the others,
when, being supposed to be excessively
sea-sick on the mimic boat on which
they were travelling, exclaimed in loud

KYRLE BELLEW.

tones, "How I wish I could land on Diamond Island and have another chowder!" accompanying his speech by an expressive glance towards our box.

This decidedly drew the attention of the house, as people suffering from *mal de mer* are not generally clamoring for chowder, and the sisters, as usual, had to come to the rescue to put a stop to any further reckless improvisations on his part.

After the play we all repaired to the "Sturtevant House" in New York, where the Vokes were stopping, and after having paid them a little call, started for our respective homes.

While waiting for a car on the "Gilsey House" corner, I thought I detected rather thick smoke issuing from the roof of the "Sturtevant," and suggested the house might be on fire. The idea was ridiculed by the remainder of the party, however, and we all went our various ways.

7

My surmise proved correct, for the next morning's papers gave us the acaount of rather a severe fire that had occurred in that hotel.

We went to inquire for the Vokes, and discovered they had not suffered anything more than a severe fright; that Victoria, upon finding the women scantily attired, and all crowding in a panic towards the ladies' entrance, had mounted a chair and delivered, off-hand, a free lecture upon the subject of self-control; that Jessie was positive the women in this country did not wear night-dresses, for she had not discovered one who was so attired; and Miss Sanson was causing unrestrained mirth on account of the peculiar assortment of things she had tried to save.

They told one little incident of Fred's experience in the general *mêlée*.

When matters were somewhat calming down at the "Sturtevant," he crossed the street to the "Gilsey

House" on some errand. Standing at the desk registering, he descried a man attired in white under-drawers, red shirt, high-top boots, and a high black hat : he was moved by the resemblance in his costume to facetiously slap him on the back, (a total stranger), jocularly remarking : "I say, old man, you're up early ; are you going hunting ?"

"Damn it !" replied the irate one addressed. "Don't you know the 'Sturtevant House' is on fire ?"

Innumerable incidents could be re-lated of these pleasant people, and it is with sincere sorrow I realize we shall never look upon their like again, for several members of the "Family" have died within the past few years, and no one who has ever seen them together would desire to see their places filled by others.

Filled they could not be, for the "Vokes Family," as they originially appeared, were entirely unique.

Could Kyrle Bellew be considered Vain?

IN days now somewhat remote, discussion at times waxed animated over a then seemingly important question, theatrically and indeed socially—"Was or was not Kyrle Bellew possessed of great vanity?" I believe the matter has never been definitely settled, though in an individual instance I recall it would seem there was some valid ground for a supposition in the affirmative.

The occasion was an informal "evening" at Mrs. Lester Wallack's, and gathered about one of the tables were two or three young ladies, Mr. Bellew and some other men.

Bellew had some bits of paper in his hands from which he was idly fashioning little boats.

"I hear," he drawled, addressing no one in particular, "that your American navy is badly in need of ships. I propose to remedy the evil by presenting you with a few."

One girl in the party spoke up quickly in slightly sarcastic vein :

"I am sure we all render sincere thanks in the name of the American navy."

The actor favored her with an especially comprehensive glance, and finishing his boat, pencilled a few words on it and patronizingly tossed it over to her.

The girl picked the boat up slowly (this was the first occasion she had met Mr. Bellew) and read—"My love to you, Kyrle Bellew." She flushed rather a vivid crimson, but, looking the young man steadily in the eyes, said in tones sufficiently clear for all to comprehend, "The sentiment inscribed here (indicating the boat) is surely too much of an honor for any one woman to aspire to, so with your permission, Mr. Bellew, I will take it home, raffle it, and—send you the proceeds." She then rose, bowed and left the table, at the same time leaving Mr. Bellew sufficiently disconcerted to bite his lip, and permit his brow the shadow of a frown.

Mr. Bellew Married or Single.

AT the height of Mr. Kyrle Bellew's reign in New York, on the stage and in the heart of the matinée-girl, when Thirtieth Street opposite "Palmer's Theatre" (where Mr. Bellew principally held sway) would be crowded every Saturday afternoon with young women belonging to the best "set" in the city waiting patiently to catch a glimpse of the actor as he issued from the stage-entrance after the performance, there was much anxious inquiry among these same misguided young females as to whether their idol was married or single. Not that a solution of the matter could affect any of them one way or the other, but a number of the younger ones, I presume, preferred to worship and dream of him in private, untrammelled by the prosaic details of family attachments. *"Anyway,"* they "wanted to know."

One of the sisterhood having an acquaintanceship with Mr. Louis James volunteered to apply to him for information, and thus have the burning question settled. Accordingly, upon the next occasion of their meeting, the young spokeswoman prided herself upon adroitly bringing the subject to the foreground. Her opinion of her own deftness suddenly vanished, however, upon being unmercifully teased by the quick-witted Mr. James, gaining no information, (he having none to give,) and with the added pang of hearing "dear Kyrle" dubbed (in a spirit of wickedness with the design of worrying his fair inquisitor), 'bandy-legged,' by the athletic actor.

But before they parted, Mr. James relented, and promised to gather all the items on the subject he could, transmitting them to her by the earliest post ;

thus, within a few days, she received from him the following :—

> '' Here's a how-de-do,
> I've found it out for you,
> When a man can live on eggs,
> He's sure to have most bandy legs,
> And then he's married too,
> Dear lovely Kyrle Bellew," etc.

Below this verse a slip clipped from a daily paper was pasted, and heavily outlined with a border of black ink. It read :

"BELLEW.—Kyrle Bellew is a married man. His wife lives in England, and he is thrifty in his personal habits. His only dissipation is his fondness for hard-boiled eggs."

After this came a second verse from Mr. James :

> "Here's a state of things,
> All hearts he's torn to strings.
> Just because dear Kyrle's not single,
> All the girls their tears will mingle.
> Poor dear Kyrle Bellew,
> Here's a how-de-do," etc.

> "After the ' Mikado '—
> "But don't despair, *I'm* still living.
> "Yours,
> "' LOUISA.'

After receiving the above, in the name

of suffering girlhood, and on bright
scarlet paper emblematic of their hearts'
blood, the recipient of the above indited
the following acknowledgment to the
tragedian :

> " Here's a pretty mess.
>   Of you we think no less,
>   But when word came he was married
>   All to their rooms were fainting carried.
>   Lives he's wrecked a few,
>   This hateful Kyrle Bellew ! " etc.

> " Ah ! this is too too much,
>   ' Bandy legs,' ' wife,' and ' hard-boiled eggs,'
>   Now we taste the bitter dregs
>   Of unrequited passion."

It may have been the newspaper item
quoted above had a more salutary effect
upon girldom than even a mother's admonition or a father's stern command,
or it is possible Mr. Bellew tired of
wholesale worship. Be this as it may,
dating from that time, the *furore*
created by his cameo-like beauty seemed
to decline, and he was allowed to settle
down with but few remonstrances as
Mrs. Potter's "leading man."

The Stage of Indifference.

IT is interesting at times to retrace one's mental steps, and determine the cause of an inspiration, no matter of what order.

Certainly " an up-to-date " farce-comedy would scarcely be sought as the legitimate cause of a serious re-ligious discussion, "between the acts," or the following verses be regarded as the outcome of such a discussion, but indulgence is craved, as the facts remain.

Two of the guests in a large theatre party given one evening to witness a sample of this popular kind of amuse-ment, certainly "got in very deep."

From dwelling upon the stupidity of prevailing "shows" (the only word adequate to the performances) and this one in particular, they advanced to the present indifference of people to things in general, the lady going so far as to remark, "That at times it almost seemed as though God had given up taking any interest in the affairs of this world."

The man replied, " Being an atheist the word God held no especial meaning for him," in fact, he would quite as soon so denominate his companion, as any one else.

She was fairly shocked at this, and told him under the circumstances he tempted her to call *him* the " Devil." Very seriously, however, the gentleman advanced his atheistic arguments, but the young lady was not to be convinced. They were interrupted by the orchestra loudly trumpeting forth " Johnny's Gun," in the midst of which choice selection, the young woman emitted a slightly hysterical laugh.

Upon her escort inquiring the cause,

she said, "It just struck me as so funny that 'God' and the 'Devil,' should be seated side by side in the theatre, and the audience remain actually indifferent to the fact."

Upon returning home from the theatre that evening, acting upon an impulse, the young lady seized her pen and indited these lines to her friend :—

"THE STAGE OF INDIFFERENCE."

TO

W. E. P. F.

" The Devil and God at the play were seen
   Side by side in the parquette chairs.
   To the rest of the audience gathered there,
   It seemed a droll and peculiar affair,
   That the moving powers of heaven and hell
   Should emerge from their respective shell,
   To meet in a spot that was not—well,
   A suitable place for either !

" Yet, though it wasn't a *usual* thing
   When the orchestra 'started up,'
   They turned their attention to things in hand,
   Such as ' Johnny's Gun ' as played by the band ;
   For, after all, we live in an age
   ' Taking things as they come ' 'twould baffle to
      guage.

Neither God nor the Devil are now the rage,
But—*La demoiselle Soubrette.*

" The Devil had donned a persuasive smile,
    Having lured God in to show him,
    Though ministers roared and tried to blight
    The lives that swarmed in the calcium light,
    There was many a beautiful spotless elf
    ' Playing her part' on that glittering shelf,
    Who like unto him, their other self,
    Was ' not so bad as *painted.*'

" But in the stage of indifference we mostly dwell,
    It's a very wearisome thing
    To be roused from that ' little world of our own,'
    And asked to judge of the seed as sown,
    To wake for the right, and a battle wage,
    In affairs either on or off the stage.
    ' None of my business,' remarks the sage,
    ' And so I'll not interfere.'

L'ENVOI.

" God watched, and listened and took it in,
    The arms and legs all waving there.
    The masses of streaming golden hair,
    The gauzy raiment an angel *might* wear ;
    Then meeting his neighbor's satanic stare
    Said, " I wish you good luck, and I
    Hope there's a leaven, still—by your leave,
    I'll *return*—to heaven.' "

Incidents in the World of Music.

THE members of the dramatic profession are frequently commended for
their general good nature and generosity
towards one another, but for some mysterious cause these qualities do not
seem to communicate themselves to the
musical branch to any great extent.
The latter art is popularly supposed to
possess charms that in some way soothe
the savage breast, and although this
may be its effect on an audience, the
opposite seems to be true of the artist,
in whom it apparently very often breeds
selfishness, vanity and irritability.

Without doubt the true musician's
nerves are in a more acute condition
than those of the rest of mankind, and
the care of a voice, at all events, would
tend necessarily towards a somewhat

selfish life. These are then the only
reasons I can offer in explanation of the
difference that exists.

I remember witnessing an instance of
the selfishness that can be displayed by
one singer towards another, and, though
a mere child at the time, its striking me
so forcibly that it created a very lasting
impression. It occurred at the "United
States Hotel," Saratoga.

Miss Clara Louise Kellogg, at the time
extremely stout, and also somewhat on
her last notes with the public, occupied
one of the "States'" cottages. Sig.
Brignoli, who, according to tradition,
had been the most fascinating and
adored of the tenors of his time, was at
Saratoga also ; not at the "States," but
at some second-rate boarding-house in
the village. "Very poor," every one
said, and sighed as they did so that this
genius should be enduring such a sor-
rowful old age.

His voice was still extremely sweet,

for he sang sometimes in the morning, (I had the pleasure of hearing him,) and also, despite everything, he had still managed to preserve to a certain extent the air of the gallant and petted favorite of other days.

One morning a party of ladies of "a certain age" were seated at a corner of the long hotel piazza, when Miss Kellogg and Brignoli happened to pass one another on the promenade, the prima donna merely according a careless nod to the latter. One of the ladies noticing this, observed that Miss Kellogg's present affluence evidently prevented her feeling the necessity of the companionship of the artist who had nothing. "And yet," she continued, "I can recall, in the days when she made her *début* and Brignoli was already a great tenor, his marked kindness to the nervous young singer. He gave her his advice and his help in a thousand different ways, then much coveted and

8

of great value to her, as I presume it has been throughout her career; but now!" and the speaker shrugged her shoulders significantly.

A few days later it was announced that Miss Kellogg would give a concert, at which, of course, all fashionable Saratoga would be expected to attend. Sig. Brignoli, upon being made aware of the event, approached the lady referred to, begging her to intercede with Miss Kellogg on his behalf to give him an engagement to sing at the same concert.

Knowing the tenor to be sadly in need of funds, and also feeling that his name would still prove a magnet to a host of his old admirers who were summering at the Spa, she very willingly undertook the mission, only however to feel thoroughly grieved and indignant over the result.

She preferred her request at the first opportunity, to which Miss Kellogg's reply was something to the effect that "she couldn't be bothered with him."

Neither was any one else "bothered" with him very long, for within a comparatively short period of the foregoing incident, he died in a top-floor room at the "Everett House" in New York, not possessed of sufficient of this world's goods to provide him with the means for a decent exit therefrom. Fortunately, towards the last, one or two of his old friends discovered his condition and made themselves responsible for the necessary expenses attending his death.

It is also pleasant to know that as his hour arrived, he seemed to lose sight of his troubles, his mind wandering back to the time of his early triumphs, and he finally expired most tranquilly, singing one of his favorite airs.

*   *   *   *   *

Occasionally you meet with a tenor who gives better attention to his exchequer than did poor Brignoli. An amusing little incident illustrating this was recounted to me by a lady who had interested herself in getting up an entertainment for charity, at which, among others Campanini had been requested to sing.

He forwarded a very polite reply to her invitation, saying he regretted exceedingly his inability to sing upon the occasion designated, but enclosed a cheque for fifty dollars, which he begged her to make use of in connection with the charity.

Delighted with his generosity, though at the same time sincerely mourning the absence it would entail of the artist, she sent him an immediate and profuse acknowledgment of the cheque.

Whether repentance for the act overtook him in the night she could not say, but the following day she received a note from the great singer by messenger, conveying the intelligence that circumstances would allow him to sing for her after all, and requesting her to kindly return him his cheque by bearer.

She laughed heartily over this donation "with a string to it," as slangy little boys would put it, but at the same time expressed her thankfulness at the exchange. "For, after all," said she, "there are plenty of fifty-dollar bills in the world, but—only *one* Campanini."

*   *   *   *   *

All *impresarios*, I believe, entertain different views upon "the way to get there." A noticeable point in Col. Henry Mapleson's policy was, that all his business transactions should bear the social stamp as well, and he continued to pursue this course in the management of his late wife, Laura Schirener-Mapleson, the prima donna, with considerable success.

He encountered many difficulties in trying to accomplish this during his

latest visit to America, because of having presented Marie Roze as his wife
upon a former occasion. Indignation
being somewhat prevalent in the higher
circles that he now repudiated the fact,
and desired Laura Schirener to be recognized as occupying the position then
held by Madame Roze.

However, he made a bold fight to over-
come all obstacles, and, together with
his own easy address, Madame Mapleson's beauty and the whispers rife of her
"interesting history," succeeded fairly,
as the first step arranging to have
Madame Mapleson sing at several
private *musicales*.

There was one lady however wield-
ing considerable social influence, who
though she thus came into contact with
the Maplesons at the houses of her
friends, vowed not to countenance them
in her own.

It is apparently not always good policy
to write yourself down too distinctly

in these matters, as was evidenced later on.

One of the large charitable entertainments of the season patronized by society was in process of erection, so to speak, in which the lady to whom I refer was deeply interested. It was suggested that doubtless Madame Mapleson would be very happy on this occasion to sing for her. The social leader thought this might be extremely possible, as it was to be a very fashionable affair, but declined to consider the artist's services.

The day before that set for the performance, the former received a message informing her that the celebrity upon whom she had been relying was suddenly obliged to leave town. Quite in despair over this catastrophe occurring at such a late hour, she hurriedly applied to every one whom she thought could possibly fill the place made vacant, but none were available at such short notice, and on every side she was advised to seek Madame Mapleson.

With rather a grim smile overspreading her face, as she recognized the finger of fate and her own defeat, she finally directed her coachman to the apartment house occupied by the Maplesons, and there, with the most gracious manner possible, preferred her request to the husband of the prima donna.

The colonel, suave and calm as usual, recognized the fact that "the lady was giving them very short notice," but he felt no doubt whatever apparently that his wife would take pleasure in accommodating her and singing for her charity with—the following proviso :

That every newspaper should announce through its columns the next morning, that "At the very last moment, and at the *request* of Mrs. ——, Madame Laura Schirener-Mapleson had kindly consented to sing," etc. A like announcement must also be made from

the stage before the performance commenced.

Groaning in spirit under the weight
of her bondage, though at the same time
realizing its justice under the circumstances, the lady accepted the colonel's
terms, outwardly with apparent good
grace.

The announcements were made as
directed, and Madam, Mapleson, beautifully attired and looking very handsome, proved a great success with her
audience.

*   *   *   *   *

To the suggestion of envy or selfishness, as existing between singers and
musicians in general, I must at all
events indicate one exception, though
undoubtedly many more exist. The
one I refer to in the present instance is
Sig. Tagliapietra, the Italian with the
glorious baritone and perfect method ;
the singer, who, to voice the sentiments

of one of the celebrated *maestros*, could have been anything he chose, or occupied any position he desired in the world of music, had he been a bit more practical, displayed more interest in his affairs, and curbed his desire for indulging in an amusement in which he found too much pleasure—horse-racing. An occupation also exacting much time and voice.

The singer has yet to be heard who can render "The Heart Bowed Down" from "The Bohemian Girl," as Tagliapietra renders it, or who can so vitalize to that thrilling degree the part of the Toreador in "Carmen." I listened to his impassioned virile personation of the latter character one night that the opera was being given, and a few evenings later met him at a private *musicale;* there, as on the stage, he sang magnificently as usual, and in both surroundings his bearing, despite the admiration excited by his talent, remained as simple and unaffected as that of a child.

In the course of the same evening, Herr Carl Streitmann, then the tenor of the " Lillian Russell Opera Company." sang several selections from " La Cigale " (the opera then being presented by the latter) most charmingly.

As he finished, it was a pleasure to watch Tagliapietra, who had been standing by the piano while the tenor sang. His " bravos " and enthusiasm were beyond others', his feelings being expressed in the most earnest and ingenuous fashion.   Not satisfied that the sweet notes should yet cease, he exclaimed, " Oh, Streitmann, sing this one for me, please," meanwhile handing Herr Streitmann the number from " La Cigale," " Trifle Not with Love."   " It is my favorite, you know," he continued, " and you sing it so beautifully." Streitmann smilingly complied, fulfilling the request in exquisite style, and upon his reaching the *finale*, Tagliapietra again lavished heartfelt and generous appreciation upon the tenor.

*   *   *   *   *

The opera comique companies are not to be distanced by their elder sisters of grand opera in their capacity for evolving disputes, contentions and enmities. No company of the kind, I think, could at one time boast of a more complicated state of affairs in this direction than the " Lillian Russell Opera Company," about the date it reached Boston on its tour through the country with " La Cigale."

Several members of the company did not attempt to screen the fact that the prima-donna 'succeeded in rendering their existence anything but a dream, and so far as the tenor and the fair diva were concerned, they had quite ceased to speak.

Though night after night as their *rôles*
in the opera demanded that they should
evince deepest love for one another, for
the benefit of their audiences, of course
they did so, but once the friendly shelter
of the " wings " was gained they re-
lapsed into contemptuous silence.   One
evening this condition of affairs was
altered for a few moments, when a
short conversation ensued in an under-
tone while they were still before the
footlights.   Streitmann was clasping
Miss Russell to his heart in a very fervor
of artistic rapture, and singing to her of
his love in the impassioned manner so
natural to him, when he suddenly heard
her say, "Take care, take care."   A
slight pause occurring he quickly inquired, *sotto voce*, " Of what ? "   " You
have turned my face away from the
audience," replied Miss Russell.

As Streitmann finished the number he
almost shoved her from him, breathing
out fiercely, " Bah ! You call yourself

an artist, and can think of such trifles as that ?"

Later on commenced what might be termed the battle of flowers.

Miss Attalie Claire, who impersonated the female *rôle* next in importance to Miss Russell's in the company, was forced to suffer some severe penalties when an impetuous though possibly ill-advised admirer began deluging the young singer and the theatre with his floral offerings in her honor, until a veto was put upon it by " the management " and then the young gentleman, determining that his action in the matter should not be wholly restrained, caused to be displayed the flowers that would otherwise have been sent to the theatre, in one of the most prominent of the "Hub's" shop-windows hired for the occasion.

The press and the people vigorously discussed the incident, thus continuing to give greater prominence to Miss

Claire than was at all relished by the head of the organization to which she belonged, and, in consequence, every trifle that could add to the former's annoyance behind the scenes was now put in practice. Finally one evening Miss Russell told the young lady she could no longer allow her to use the blonde wig she had been wearing in her part, as it interfered with the effect of the prima donna's own light hair.

All were small matters in their way, but the wig proved the culminating straw, and Miss Claire proceeded to behave in truly feminine fashion, first by crying bitterly, and then fainting dead away.

However, though at one time productive of tears and discomfort, the flowers finally proved to be Miss Claire's pathway to the altar, for, shortly after her season with Miss Russell closed, she became the wife of the very wealthy young man who had unwittingly increased her troubles by his attentions, and retired with him to private life.

*   *   *   *   *

The advertising methods resorted to by the managers of that most difficult of all things to manage, a prima donna, are wonderful and varied. "Losing their diamonds," being followed by non-repressible admirers, accidents and robberies, all are resorted to; but among the most ingenious and unique inventors of these necessary little booms stands Mr. James W. Morrissey.

For some time he directed the fortunes of the late Miss Emma Abbott, whose great popular success throughout the country was very largely attributable to the wonderful manner in which he kept her before the public. Miss Abbott was neither beautiful nor particularly attractive in any way; she was far from being a great artist in grand opera, and yet—she drew crowded

DION BOUCICAULT in "The Shaughraun."

houses, and died possessed of large wealth.

"The Abbott stage kiss" became famous, for what reason, and in what way, one would have to apply for particulars to Mr. Morrissey.

The prima-donna herself was possessed of extraordinary energy and push, and, in combination with her manager, who more than equalled her in these characteristics, they usually found themselves on the "top wave."

During one period of her operatic career the New York papers were filled with the details of a murder which a man and woman were jointly accused of committing. The pair had stood two trials, and were still proclaiming their innocence of the deed, and calling for a third, though they had not the means for paying the expenses of the same.

Ever on the alert, Mr. Morrissey's quick brain recognized here an opportunity for his prima donna. Accord-

9

ingly he suggested to Miss Abbott that *she* should raise the necessary amount to cover the expenses of a third trial, by "soliciting subscriptions." No sooner resolved upon than put into practice; Miss Abbott and Mr. Morrissey immediately engaged a carriage, and entering it, list in hand, drove to the various offices of the prominent merchants and brokers, obtaining the sums requested with so little trouble, that before two o'clock, Miss Abbott had collected one thousand and ten dollars—a sum sufficient to cover the expenses of a third trial for these poor wretches. She enclosed to them one thousand dollars, and then, feeling somewhat hungry and fatigued after her morning's work, used the extra ten in paying for a little lunch at Delmonico's which was shared by her genial manager, during the progress of which they did not forget to drink to the success and good health of the prisoners.

The following morning the papers were filled with admiration and wonder over the charity and kind heart of Miss Emma Abbott, and, as the story gradually filtered through the profession, you may be sure Mr. Morrissey's services as a manager were in greater demand than ever.

Mr. Henry Irving's "Lyceum Theatre" Court.

THE public is of course generally aware that much ceremony attaches to the Court of St. James, presided over as it is by her Royal Highness, Queen Victoria, but I doubt if they have equal knowledge of that exacted from the court surrounding her distinguished theatrical subject, Mr. Henry Irving, in his London theatre, the ''Lyceum.''

Several years since, the late Lawrence Barrett consummated arrangements with Mr. Irving by which he and his company should occupy the "Lyceum" during a summer season.

The final arrangements being completed, the Barrett company set sail for '' the other side,'' arriving in London a week before the close of Mr. Irving's

season, and the opening of their own,
and feeling naturally curious concern-
ing the inner workings of the theatre
tenanted by the best-known actor of
his day, the more prominent members
of the company, taking advantage of
Mr. Irving's invitation, made themselves at home both before and behind
the curtain.

All the surroundings seemed calcu-
lated to inspire awe ; the attendants
and *attachés* were drilled like soldiers,
and there was a tendency among them
to lower their tones to the pitch regarded
as canonical when entering a church.
Perfect order reigned, and all had the
name of Irving upon their lips as though
referring to some supreme deity.

The crowning touch of impressiveness
was given by the following ceremony :

Before a door which some one whis-
pered to you was " Mr. Irving's dressing-
room," stood a boy in rigidly upright
position, whose duty in general was to

guard his master from any sudden approach from the outside world, and in particular he was known as Mr. Irving's private "call-boy."

A moment before the actor's "cue" would be given for his entrance on the stage, the general "call-boy" would approach the former and intimate the fact.

The private "call-boy" then giving a discreet tap, to which the door would be opened, imparted this information to Mr. Irving, and then the youth advancing, with Mr. Irving following in his wake, would make his way to the former's stage entrance, waving his arms as though to disperse any real or imaginary impediment, and at the sametime crying—

"Make way for Mr. Irving."

"Make way for Mr. Irving."

In this royal fashion, Mr. Irving would be finally ushered before his audience.

" Adonis " Dixey's Offhand Estimate of himself.

THE ingenuous view which our friend " Adonis " Dixey takes of his own admixture of brain and tissue is concisely illustrated by his reply to a comparative stranger who was suggesting his adaptability for a piece in which his Majesty, Satan, was the leading light.

" Ah, yes ! " responded " Adonis " D. " I've frequently been told I ought to personate the 'Devil,' I'm such a h——l of a fellow."

A Playright's Interview with the Mansfield.

FROM "Adonis" D. to Richard Mansfield, is, theatrically speaking, a stride, but the subject-matter *vanitas*—riots along through the veins of both in equally healthy fashion, possibly with the odds in Richard's favor, making them—kin.

A little anecdote is related of the latter who, though of course the central figure, played his part upon this occasion, at least, nearly "out of sight."

The puppets on the scene were a modest playwright, possessed, for a wonder, of an acknowledged good play, and Mrs. Mansfield—the latter on behalf of, and the honored mouth-piece of, Richard. The "m. p." (modest playwright) not being yet sufficiently innoculated to enter direct to the holy of holies, *i. e.*, Richard's presence.

Evidently bearing in mind the copybook maxim of "Honesty," etc., the playwright began the interview by stating that the piece in question had been allowed to go *en tour* in Canada, but had not been exploited in the United States.

Saturated with the importance of her mission, Mrs. Mansfield raised her right hand in token of disapproval—"Nothing further need be said," she remarked, "for, had you the finest play ever written, Mr. Mansfield would not touch it; *he* must create the *rôle* always, no one else can have had anything to do with it;" then, with a deprecatory smile, "with the exception, of course of those in Shakespearean productions, and their having been written so many years ago could hardly have been helped."

Just here Richard appeared and disappeared at an open door, a dissolving vision in a quilted jacket, as though to ratify the rites.

It was over—and the "m. p.," filled with a strange reproachful irritability towards the immortal William for having lived too soon, was silently let down six flights in an elevator, feeling it was only *half* as far as deserved.

A Realistic Dream of the Late Lester Wallack.

DREAMS in general are of no especial
interest to any one, unless it be to the
dreamer, who experiences a certain
sense of importance in relating them
the following morning to a select audience whose hair may obligingly stand
on end with horror, or whose ear may
be charmed, according to the subject-
matter, but occasionally you hear of
one that impresses you, and the following, given to me as authentic, may
arrest attention, if only for the reason
that it has for its central figure that
of the late Lester Wallack.

Within the year after Mr. Wallack's
death a movement was inaugurated
having for its object the raising of sufficient funds by popular subscription to

erect a statue in bronze of the well-
known actor ; the same to be placed,
when finished, in a suitable part of the
city (New York).

An appeal was framed and issued "To
the Public," setting forth therein the
many good reasons for the erection of
such a statue, and signed by thirty-four
of New York's most prominent society
women, Messrs. August Belmont & Co.
graciously accepting to act as bankers.

In consideration of the immense popularity of Wallack, and " Wallack's
Theatre," it seemed impossible that the
project should meet with anything but
complete success.

Alas for the surety of human au-
guries !

After the first few hundred dollars
were subscribed, in some inexplicable
way, the gracious work seemed to fall
through of its own weight.

This proved a great disappointment
to many, particularly so to personal

friends of the Wallack family who had deeply interested themselves. Among the latter was a young lady who had been appointed the secretary and who had worked very earnestly for success.

Before such an idea as failure, however, had been contemplated, the principal thought exercising her mind was *which* of Wallack's numerous stage characters should be selected to most fittingly represent him in bronze.

No one seemed able to decide, not even St. Gaudens, who, by popular voice, was to be the sculptor.

One day, while paying Mrs. Wallack a visit, the young secretary suggested what a boon it would be could Mr. Wallack settle the matter for them, "for," added she, "in that clean-cut graceful, decisive way of his, he would decide in an instant, and to perfection."

As is often the case with a vexed question, it haunts one with maddening persistency, seeming as though for

its own sake, it sought a solution ; and
so it was the young lady could not
seem to free herself from this one.

Seating herself at the piano the same
evening, she sought, by playing over
some of Mr. Wallack's favorite ballads
—"If My Glances should Betray Me,"
sung in "Rosedale," "Once Again,"
and so on, to gain some distinct impression, but, as may be supposed, nothing of a supernatural nature occurred,
and at last, vaguely disappointed, she
retired for the night.

The following morning, however, she
awakened rather suddenly, and sat up
with that bewildered sensation of some
strong, all-pervading presence that
sometimes marks the line between
waking and dreaming as indistinct.

She had an engagement with Mrs.
Wallack that day, and, upon meeting
her, said, "Before anything else, let me
tell you of a dream I had last night of
Mr. Wallack. I call it a dream, and

yet it was so vivid, so real, that even yet I cannot shake off its effect.

"At first," she proceeded, "I seemed to find myself in a long, dark street with no distinguishing features ; but, as I proceeded, I came upon a large building I recognized as a theatre, and before what was apparently a side door, over which hung a swinging-lamp, stood Mr. Wallack talking to an attendant. No one else was in sight.

"I walked directly up to him, telling him I had come to see him, though my purpose only seemed to reveal itself to me at the moment. He replied—'Yes, my dear, I know it, I was expecting you; and now come inside at once, for though the night is warm, I am very chilly.'

"The servant, for such he seemed to be, with lighted torch, preceded us through a chain of beautiful, low-ceiled rooms hung in rich stuffs, finally arriving at the farthest one, an oriental-looking place done in ruby velvet and heavy gold, with lights glittering everywhere like jewels.

"As we stood in the middle of this apartment, I said rather sadly to Mr. Wallack, 'You know I have come to bid you good-bye.' 'Yes,' he replied, 'I know—we shall never meet again—*here.*' I felt tears spring to my eyes, and as he rested one hand lightly on my shoulder, with the evident intention of comforting me, there came to us suddenly the sound as of a mighty clapping. 'Hark!' said he, as he raised his other hand in a listening gesture, then, with a satisfied look upon his face, he continued, 'Ah, there is a great house to-night, the largest I have ever played to; but,' he added, as with a sigh his hand slipped from my shoulder, 'it is for the last time,— I shall never play again.' Then rallying, and again addressing me, he said, 'They are clapping for me to appear, you know; so I must not keep them

JAMES W. MORRISSEY.

waiting, and now little one—a long good-bye.' And so we parted.

"The torch-bearer preceded me as before, and, feeling very grave and sad, I followed him until we had almost reached the entrance, when I turned to gain my last look at Mr. Wallack.

"The tableau that rewarded me caused me to catch my breath in admiration. Under a great sunburst of light that irradiated everything in a dazzling, unearthly manner, in the centre of the ruby-and-gold room he stood, attired in the full white flowing robes of an Arab chieftain, and gleaming out against the red drapery of the room as though hewn from marble, so handsome, so chiselled.

"Would that St. Gaudens could have seen him at that moment, and had he been but half true to the original, he would have created a work of art that would have been a delight for all time."

10

Having finished the details of her dream, the young secretary, in a puzzled tone, asked Mrs. Wallack what she made of it all, saying, that though Mr. Wallack made a magnificent picture to her mind in the dress, still she could not see why he should have been costumed like an Arab.

Mrs. Wallack, without replying, rose and requested the young lady to follow her into an adjoining room, then pointing out a very large, full-length photograph of Mr. Wallack in the garb of an Arab chieftain, asked quietly, "Was it anything like that?"

" Why, that is it," gasped her astonished visitor.

" Have you never seen 'The Veteran,' one of Mr. Wallack's favorite characters?" queried Mrs. Wallack.

"Never!" replied the young lady. "Indeed I don't ever remember hearing of it."

"Under those circumstances," mused

Mrs. Wallack, " it seems very peculiar for you to have had this dream. I wonder," she continued, " this character did not occur to me as the one from which to model the statue, not, however, in this Arabian costume, but in his own short kilt and open shirt, worn before he changed with the Arab. The difficulty now will be to obtain a photograph of him in that costume. I have none, and cannot tell you who has, unless possibly Sarony."

The dream, however, decided the choice of character for the statue, for the secretary, nothing daunted by Mrs. Wallack's reference to the difficulty of obtaining the photograph, spent some days in seeking it in the different galleries and private collections. Finally in one of the latter she secured it, and took it immediately to St. Gaudens, who pronounced it the perfection of poses, as indeed it was, and a vast pity it is that this beautiful work of art, as

it would doubtless have been had the
necessary fifteen thousand dollars for
its completion been forthcoming, is not
commanding "Players' Square."

Signor Brignoli on a Railway Train.

THE ruling passion of a tenor strong in death (his voice) was exemplified by Signor Brignoli one afternoon on a railway train.

He was touring through the country with the "Parepa Rosa Concert Co.," which included, besides the ladies, Ferranti, Jules Levy, the famous cornet player, and Mr. James W. Morrissey as treasurer for the company.

Their next stopping-place was to be Meadeville, Penn., where they intended giving a concert that evening. Brignoli, always hospitably inclined, leaned over towards Mr. Morrissey, a few miles before reaching their destination, and invited the latter to dine with him upon their arrival, a courtesy accepted by the treasurer with pleasure.

Approaching within sight of the depot, every one stood up, gathering their wraps together or putting them on, when the train suddenly gave a violent lurch before coming to a standstill, flinging Brignoli, who was standing in the aisle, flat on his face.

As he fell, he exclaimed, in his broken English, "I am keeled! I am keeled!" But he gradually dragged himself to a standing position near the door, to which he clung with his left hand, while he convulsively grasped at his chest with his right, and, regardless of the fact as to whether every bone in his body might not be broken, sang several bars of the tenor's prison solo from "Trovatore" in his usual exquisite style, ejaculating as he finished—Thank God! Thank God! The voice is still there. Come on, Morrissey, let us go and dine."

James W. Morrissey's Musical Congress under the Patronage of Dom Pedro II.

DURING the "Centennial" year at Philadelphia, James W. Morrissey was, for the time being, principally engaged in booming "Decker Brothers'" pianos. It was not exactly in his line of business—but then the methods of making bread and butter are not always matters of choice. At the time mentioned, the pianos were not going out, or the bread and butter coming in as rapidly as seemed desirable, and as necessity is surely the mother of invention, it occurred to the versatile manager, that a "Musical Congress" combining a series of concerts, which would include the best talent procurable, and at which the Decker pianos would be used, as a matter of course, would be the greatest advertisement for the latter that could be conceived at the moment. For Mr. Morrissey to think is to act, and within a very short time his plans for the above were formed and he had obtained the names of Clara Louise Kellogg, Annie Louise Cary, Mme. Zelda Seguin, Signor Brignoli, Remmertz, Ferranti, and a host of equally celebrated and popular artists for his programme.

Dom Pedro (the Emperor of Brazil), and his suite having arrived in Philadelphia, it also occurred to the enthusiastic head of this musical enterprise if he could arrange to give it under the patronage of the emperor it would add very materially to its lustre and brilliancy. He accordingly obtained an audience with Dom Pedro, and preferred his request, which was most graciously granted. At the same time Mr. Morrissey begged to place a box at the emperor's disposal for each concert.

The emperor said he should be delighted to attend the performances, being extravagantly fond of music, but he must be allowed the privilege of paying for his own box, which he did, sending for it regularly every morning as long as the affair lasted. Upon the occasion of the opening night, the Academy was decorated from pit to dome with flags, drapery and flowers, the emperor's box, of course, being most lavishly done up. A vast audience filled every seat and niche of standing-room, the previous advertising having been accomplished in the most discreet and attractive manner. Dom Pedro and suite were in his box, the programme was being fulfilled in more than satisfactory fashion, and Mr. Morrissey, content with what he had so far achieved, was standing in the lobby near the box-office, conversing with some friends, when he heard his name pronounced. Turning his

head he found himself confronted by a
man attired in a magnificent uniform,
and whom he recognized as one of the
royal aides. The latter proffered him
a note, remarking at the same time,
"From the emperor."

The manager hastily opened the pen-
ciled message from royalty, in which
he found he was requested, if it were
not too late, to have a number designated as a Chopin Waltz on the programme altered to List's Rhapsodie,
No. 2, and signed, "Dom Pedro."

Mr. Morrissey instantly sent a messenger back on the stage to Julia Rivé
the pianiste, asking her not to appear
until he had spoken with her, then, requesting the aide to follow him, they
went behind the scenes and made the
necessary explanation to the artiste.

On the way "back," the emperor's note
presented the idea of a "magnificent
ad." to the managerial mind, but suppressing the desire of using it for any

such purpose until he had received a proper sanction, he turned to the aide, saying, "I would like the emperor's permission to read his note to the audience, as it seems to be due them, as well as to Mme. Rivé, to account for the change in the programme."

The aide replying that the responsibility would be his, Mr. Morrissey, nothing loath, stepped before the footlights and read the note aloud. Cheer after cheer arose from the great audience, and when Mme. Rivé appeared and rendered the selection " by request," the emperor rose, and remained standing during the entire number, at the finish sending the artiste a beautiful floral offering. The enthusiasm of the public seemed boundless.

Subsequently Decker Brothers and Mr. Morrissey realized the substantial benefit that may accrue from the pencilled lines of an emperor.

Letter and Lines from Louis James.

I THINK, from all accounts, it must have been at the time of the "silly season" so called, or, in other words, during the summer vacation, that Mr. Louis James' superabundant vitality and boyish love of fun, found their most natural vent. At all events it is about this time that those who have the privilege of his acquaintance hear of most of the tragedian's pranks.

The same young girl who made inquiries of him in reference to Kyrle Bellew's married or single state, had occasion to send a note to Mr. James the ensuing summer, from the watering-place at which she was quartered, and when his reply arrived, laughingly acceded to my request for its possession, in revenge, she suggested, for the blow he had dealt the Bellew matinée-girl contingent by giving confirmations of the former's connubial state ; adding it would be fun to make the tragedian quake by seeing his nonsense exposed to the critical public.

I give the letter in full, not in " revenge," but as amusing ; also some lines attached to a photograph of himself, which arrived at the same time. The photograph presented Mr. James in evening dress, his head adorned with a very becoming short, crisp white wig. It was as he appeared in an act of "One of our Girls," during the single season, of late years, that he lapsed from tragedy to comedy, at the " Lyceum " theatre, New York.

He, by the way, received a very goodly share of homage from the matinée-girl during that winter, always insisting, however, that it was all due to his curly white wig.

But to the letter now, which is dated
from a spot on the Massachusetts coast.

" DEAR —— :

" ' As unto the bow the cord is, so unto man is
woman.' The relation you bear *us* is even of
a stronger and more tenacious nature than the
attachment of the aforesaid cord to the ditto
bow.

" I presume you are the queen of the region you
at present inhabit, and many a poor fellow looks
upon your rosy cheek and killing eye wondering
who will draw the prize. Now don't permit any
mere summer adorer to aspire to the place I hold
in your heart of hearts ; don't be a fickle child, but
take example by me and keep your ' heart true to
Poll.'

" We are enjoying our ' *otium cum dig,*' whatever that may be, and adding to our *avoirdupois ;*
covering our ' neck-bones ' so that *décolleté*
dresses may be worn without fear of showing up
salt-cellars and the *Bony-part* family to an unsym-
pathetic public.

" Speaking of that, I'm having a ' sweet thing '
made in dresses, I can tell you,—a delicate wine-
colored foulard with under-vest *à la* ' Man.'
Revers of lace, and ruffled underskirt to waist of
same. Hat to match, made of straw and lace.

" And, oh, you dear thing, I forgot. I'm having
a new ' Mother Hubbard ' made. It's lavender,
with fluffs of lace down the front, insertion of lace
in the yoke, lace flounces, and the *loveliest* thing
in petticoats you have ever seen—*all* lace (Spanish)
to the waist, so when I raise my dress *slightly*, I'm

simply a dream. No stockings, just legs tinted to match lavender ' Hub.' *Don't* scorn a Mamma Hubbard; if you knew the comforts of a good aforesaid, you'd never be without one.

" I wear my hair short (being short, alas, of that article in spots). It's the fashion now, besides it's comfortable in hot weather, and, moreover, it is economical, as it saves wear and tear on hair-brushes.

" You remember Mrs. Wrinkle, dear, do you? Well—she's bought a new phaeton! Now we *all* know the condition of her finances, so the question naturally arises at our quiet resort—' WHERE does the money come from?'

"I'm not at all curious, as you know, but it would content me much to discover particulars.

"This spot is so distressingly healthy, ' no ills that flesh is heir to ' seem to find us out. I am happy to say we are all blooming, and that I, the ' Poor Zingara Girl' am a bud of much promise, though I fear fated to blush unseen by the eye of man.

" To your household I send a heart full of love ; kiss Jack for me. Cruel thing ! he never allows me that privilege any more—O God ! There was a time— Alas ! 'tis past. If he won't accept, kick him, a good swift one.

" Be good, say your prayers and *rest*, is the command of yours in a state of holy bliss——

"The giddy
" LOUISA."

The following, are the " lines" referred to.

" As on this sylph-like form you gaze,
　　Whom Nature true assigns,
Not only as the *Counterfeit*,
　　But author of these lines.

" Do you observe my lovely eye,
　　The sternness of my look ?
' Twas owing to a flirting fly
　　That buzzed as I was ' took.'

" He flew about my *wig-ged* head,
　　Then lit upon my nose,
And at one time, I really thought
　　We'd surely come to *blows*.

" When in my grave-clothes, I'm ' laid out,'—
　　And you this ' pictur ' see,
Oh, drop a silent tear, sweet maid
　　And sometimes think of me ! "

Tbe Influence Exercised by a White Satin Tea=Gown upon tbe Opening of a Tbeatre.

FOR those who have held their doubts, the following incident cannot fail to convince that "petticoat government" is no myth, possibly emphasized when it is a "thing of beauty."

The sterner sex have been known to loudly proclaim the joy they experience in one place at least on this troubled sphere where they rule supreme—their clubs; that only there are they exempt from the exactions of woman, lovely woman !

But are they ?

She may not be *en evidence*, yet there is always a "poper behind the throns," even in men's clubs, and I think, as usual, we may "*cherchez la*

11

femme, with the same surety of success in finding her.

With what scorn would the two thousand and odd brawny members of a prominent organization receive the proposition that a woman's filmy white satin and lace " tea-gown," could be an important factor in the opening of a magnificent building erected with the one purpose in view of furnishing them with amusement, and of exclusively sheltering their own manly forms ?

Surprising as it may be for them to realize it, such upon one occasion was the fact.

The Manhattan Athletic Club of New York City having attained the membership given above and built for themselves a magnificent club-house on Madison Avenue, decided, upon completion of the latter, to hold a " housewarming" on its stately premises, that they might give their friends and the public some idea of their palatial surroundings before taking possession. The principal feature of amusement suggested for the occasion being a theatrical performance to bo given in the beautiful little theatre attached to the club proper. The talent collected for this, consistde of about thirty men, members of the club, and as nothing was to be spared that would lend *éclat* to the affair, it was decided to have a burlesque written expressly for them.

Accordingly, upon the decision being rendered, the president of the committee on theatricals, set himself immediately to work to find the playwright who would satisfy their requirements.

The only people he thought of applying to were men whom he knew of in the profession, but in every instance there seemed to be some good reason why these could not accept the commission.

The time now lacked but six or seven weeks to the date fixed upon for the opening of the club, and growing desperate one day in the realization of the fact that the most expert writer must be given a fair opportunity to materialize good work, he called upon Mr. James W. Morrissey, the genial manager (at that time) of the "Madison Square Garden" and "Garden Theatre," and asked to be directed by him to some one upon whom he could rely to carry out his plan. To his surprise, Mr. Morrissey gave him the address of a lady, saying, if any one could do it, she could if she would.

The president of theatricals took the address offered him, though, as he afterwards confessed, in a very doubting spirit. But needs must when necessity drives, and so, within the hour he was inquiring of the lady's maid for her mistress.

The lady, who was young, and prominent in the world of society, having just returned from a tour of the summer watering-places, sat surrounded by her trunks, the unpacking of which she was superintending, when the servant, who had admitted the gentleman, announced that "some one from Mr. Morrissey desired to see her."

Having business relations with the manager, she quickly decided he had sent her some word by messenger, and seizing a white satin and lace "tea-gown," the most convenient garment within reach, hastily donned it, and descended to the drawing-room.

To her surprise, in place of the usual messenger she expected to find, a very handsome young man, attired in correct morning costume, rose and introduced himself.

After some preamble, he said he had come to ask her to write a burlesque to be used for the opening of the "Manhattan Athletic Club" house, at the same time offering Mr. Morrissey's name as a credential.

"But," objected the young lady, "I do not understand why Mr. Morrissey suggested your coming to me for such a purpose, as I have never written a burlesque, and I do not think it would be wise of me to emulate the self-confident Irishman, who, though never having played on a violin, decided he could if he tried. Besides," she added conclusively, "I have not done any work except for 'professionals,' and you must not feel offended if I suggest that, from all I have ever heard of amateurs, I should prefer not to enter that field."

"Well, you see," urged the young gentleman, "many of our men have been considered the best actors in the 'Columbia Dramatic' (the most prominent amateur society in the city), and you would find them quite different from the usual run." He then added very impressively, "Do consent, for I am perfectly certain you can write the burlesque if you only will."

"I don't see how you can be certain of anything of the kind," retorted she, "never having met me before in your life."

"Still," he observed, with possibly a trace of apology in his tone, "I feel impressed that you can, and beg you will agree to it."

After much more of the same persuasive order, and apparent blind faith in her power to accomplish anything to which she "set her mind," though somewhat wondering at the trust placed in her capacity by an entire stranger to accomplish what was, after all, something to which was attached no small responsibility, she agreed, that being Saturday, to take the matter under consideration until Monday at the same hour, when the young manager promised to return and receive her final answer.

"If by any chance," said the young playwright, "an appropriate and convincing plot occurs to me in the interim, that is, one that is strikingly original, and will carry itself, I will undertake it, if not—I shall decline."

The young gentleman then took his departure, assuring her, before he left, of his entire belief that she would be successful.

Upon finding herself alone, the object of this sudden influx of faith at first decided she had been extremely lacking in common sense for having promised to regard the matter seriously. "For it is preposterous, after all," mused she, "for me to dream of writing a thing of this kind, providing the music, and having it on the stage in six weeks from the present date." As the last thought forced its way in upon her, she experienced a sensation of panic, and prepared to despatch a note to the club immediately, containing her declination ; but she hesitated, and thereby committed herself to the hardest six weeks' labor of her life, for late on the ensuing Sunday afternoon, after continuous thinking, an absolute inspiration seemed to come to her, and dashing down the thoughts as they took form, she finally came to a stop at the bottom of her seventh page of foolscap, realizing, as she did so, that she had the outlines for a plot such as was required.

When her visitor was announced on Monday morning, she was prepared for him, MS. in hand, and, after reading it aloud, was convinced by his excessive enthusiasm that she had more than realized his wishes. So, without further parley, contracts were drawn up, and the young authoress commenced her work.

For six weeks she labored unceasingly, in reality, day and night. As soon as the first act was finished it was put in rehearsal, she of course immediately proceeding with the second.

Nothing was spared by the club in the way of expense ; the scenery was painted by the best professional scenic artists, the costumes fashioned by a prominent costumer, and all the professional coaches employed necessary for the burlesque itself, and the incidental singing and dancing, notwithstanding the great weight of the affair, fell first on the playwright and on the president of theatricals.

The latter coming every day to consult with the former, receive finished MS. and so on, found her always forging ahead, sustained by the grim determination to keep her contract to the letter ; in fact, more than keep it, for, besides writing the burlesque and lyrics, choosing the greater part of the music and composing the remainder, she attended almost all rehearsals, led the chorus (upon finding they remained very inefficient and spiritless under professional training), and consulted in the business details.

The young man afterwards confessed that undertaking the management of thirty male amateurs proved a greater task than he had imagined, and fifty times he was on the point of giving up the whole thing in sheer despair, and probably would have done so, had it not been for the encouragement and support he received from the young authoress, who never allowed the suggestion of failure to be made after she had given her final decision to undertake the work.

The gratification of success was theirs, however, though the tension was strained almost to the breaking point to accomplish it.

The burlesque was produced with every detail perfected on the night first designated, and not only fullfilled its mission of opening the house, but was pronounced a great success, being given upon many subsequent occasions, and always meeting with the same reception.

At the close of the evening, while congratulations were in order, the president of theatricals intimated to the playwright that he had a confession to make, preluding by asking her if she knew or could guess how the burlesque had come to be written.

She replied she did, for without any apology being offered for her language, she thought she might honestly say—" by the sweat of her brow."

"No, no," hastily interrupted the young gentleman, "not that. I know how very hard you worked, but I mean the *cause* of your writing it at all ?"

She suggested if he was offering her a conundrum she "gave it up."

"Well," said he, in rather shame-faced fashion, "when Morrissey gave me the address of a *lady*, I jumped to the conclusion that, through absolute necessity, for the next six weeks I should be forced into constant communication with a stern-visaged, elderly 'blue-stocking,' and the relief was so great when you came flying downstairs, attired in that white satin gown, that I determined, then and there, you should write the burlesque, and I would not accept 'no' for answer."

"Then," said the nonplussed young woman, after an instant's pause to recover from her astonishment, "your extreme desire for me to write it, and supreme faith in my powers, was not due to the impression I made upon you, of superior intelligence, but rather to the beauty and becomingness of my 'tea-gown?'"

"I'm afraid that's about it," reluctantly admitted the young president.

It seemed so ludicrous that a pretentious undertaking, such as the

one just accomplished, backed by a
dignified body of over two thousand
men, should have hung upon a thing
so frail as a concoction of satin and
lace, and the susceptibility of one individual for the same, that the playwright indulged in a ringing laugh,
rather to the dismay of her companion.

"Well!" said she, finally, "as it
happened, your luck was uppermost,
and everything has turned out satis-
factorily ; but it strikes me your decision was a risky one, and I advise
you, for the peace of your future existence in the club, not to acknowledge
to the rest of its members the influence
that was brought to bear upon them
by a white satin 'tea-gown.' "

Whistling as a Fine Art.

IT is foolish in these kaleidoscopic days of the nineteenth century, for any one to present, or try to preserve a decided taste or opinion in reference to anything or anybody. Having done so, possibly the first day of January, one may be obliged to feel disgusted and privately contemptuous of one's self by the first day of February, upon discovering they have been influenced by the popular voice, and are floating with the current as rapidly as the rest. If you are not, you might as well be, for, to be paradoxical, the "still small voice" you feebly raise to stem the tide is drowned by the roar of the multitude before its message can reach the ear.

In point of fact, the sheep will

continue to follow, unknowing, and uncaring, bleating and blocking up the highway so long as any one chooses to take the trouble to lead.   Let us not be making invidious comparisons, however, because, after all, the person who "breaks ground" in a new field, and ploughs straight through to victory, is certainly, to borrow a delightful expression from the sporting world, "clear sand,"—more especially when the person happens to be a member of the gentler sex, and therefore, perhaps, should not have the nature of the tools employed too closely scrutinized.

But even the meekest of us who have been cowed into submission, and been forced to degenerate in our ideas and desire for true art, by the *fin de siecle* caterer of amusements, who, much like the western tavern hosts of old, with pistol pointed at the first one of his cowering guests who dared to murmur against his rations, making use at the

same time of the now historic remark,
"You'll eat your hash, and you'll like
it too," occasionally get possessed with
the absurd idea of entering a protest
against the bizarre drapery with which
the goddess is frequently adorned ?

I must confess the latter portion of
the western host's remark did not fulfil itself with many of us upon the occasion of a certain *musicale* given one
evening several years ago, at the house
of a great music-lover.   Up to a certain hour, the programme rendered,
for a house concert, had been simply remarkable and artistic beyond criticism.
One celebrated artist after another had
added to the enjoyment of the guests,
who were fairly wide-eyed with astonishment over the feast offered them
by their hostess.   But, to go back for a
little, a day or two before the date of
her *musicale*, the latter had received a
note from one of the stockholders of the
"Metropolitan Opera House," whose

12

taste in music of the higher order she had faith in, asking if her programme for the coming event was full, and if not, he would send her some one who would be " *sui generis*," a lady, whose accomplishment he would leave her to display as a surprise.

Though the programme was already perfected, this mysterious offer was accepted by the hostess because of the reliance she placed in her correspondent.

To return to the evening in question, after some charming selections had been rendered, there came a little lull before the other artists present should appear, and the hostess, considering this a propitious time for developing the so-called surprise, approached a handsome-looking woman, who had entered late, smiling, and with a slight hesitation, she said, " I presume this is Mrs. Shaw ; you must pardon me, I do not know what it is you do, but this seems the right moment for doing it."

Mrs. Shaw promptly responded, "I whistle."

The hostess checked her astonishment, and the sensation of having received a cold *douche*, as promptly as possible, and making the best of things, led the performer to the piano, at the same time quietly making the announcement to her guests of what they were about to hear.

Her own fortitude could not, however, prevent the chill that crept through the long drawing-rooms, or stop the significant glances exchanged, implying the bad taste of introducing any such diversion as the present one offered, nor did the temperature regain its tropical warmth until an Italian tenor in high favor sang forgetfulness of all else into the souls of his audience.

Such was the absolute impression created at the time of Mrs. Shaw's society *début* as a whistler.

It may be her accomplishment, like

olives, became an acquired taste; at all events her triumph and success have been indisputable, and has proved the means of her earning a handsome living for herself and others.

I cannot see that any difference has been made in the treatment of hers and the most divine art—for has she not shared, equally with the expounders of the latter, the tribute and distinction of special audience before crowned heads, concerts where the public paid a guinea, and two guineas to listen to her; and have not most of the people who criticized her at the time of her *début*, forgotten their cynical remarks of the first of January and succumbed to the February thaw?

The Drawing=room Entertainer with Pro= fessional Aspirations.

BEWARE of the aspiring drawing-room entertainer who desires to effect his or her appearance before the footlights by way of the private entrance offered by some guileless hostess impregnated with the worthy desire of entertaining her friends, and, at the same time, giving the unknown genius "a lift."

Such is the burden of the wail of one aggrieved woman who has occasionally opened her portals too wide, and has, in consequence, realized several bitter fiascos occasioned by these same self-styled geniuses. These dire results also having engendered an icy distrust of the taste and knowledge of certain of those among her friends who have enthusiastically foisted their monstrosi- ~

ties of art upon her and her unsuspecting guests. '

Embittered as she now is by her experiences, her invariable reply to all later applicants of like order is the same as that uttered by Mr. Poe's "Raven," "Never More !"

Although fully appreciating her cause for feeling disturbed, I could not restrain my mirthful emotions over her account of one of the persons who, as she termed it, had made her drawing-room for the time being ridiculous. She had received a note during the "season" from one of her friends informing her of their accidental discovery of "a prodigy, a wonder." A woman possessed of a voice which, as soon as it received a proper hearing, would electrify the public;" adding that, should she desire, they would endeavor to secure her for one of the elaborate " At Homes " for which her house was celebrated.

Enthusiastic to claim this rising "star" as her own, she lost no time, but sent an immediate acceptance of her friend's offer, doubled her invitations for the occasion, and meantime felt unequal to the task of occasionally suppressing the triumphant thought that she was possibly on the eve of presenting a second Patti to a grateful public.

The night of the "At Home" had arrived, and with it a crush of her most cultured and expectant friends and acquaintances; the evening was growing a little old, and a feeling of uneasiness was commencing to spread among the guests that they might, after all, be deprived of the promised treat, when the butler announced the name of the expected one, which, from motives of good-nature, I now suppress.

The hostess moved eagerly forward to greet her prize, a dark-haired woman, whose jetty tresses were worn rather ostentatiously, bound with broad bands of red velvet in a sort of Græco-Roman fashion.

A white gown of the artistically draped order shrouded her somewhat lengthy figure, the *ensemble* creating a suspicion of labored effect, (not usually employed in society by the true artiste) upon the minds of the initiated, but rather dazzling on the whole to those whose point of view is usually restricted by the tall hedge surrounding individuals in private life.

It was evident from the first flow of eloquence, quite unrestrained or abashed by the fact of being a stranger and the cynosure of many eyes, that this long-stemmed floweret would never blush unseen or unheard, of her own volition.

She volubly inquired, "If she was late? Had she kept them waiting?" remarking that she had come as soon as she could possibly tear herself away from the house of another well-known

society woman, but where she had re-
sisted all entreaties to sing; having
saved herself for the present occasion.
Not even had she been prevailed upon
to give her clamoring friends that
charming ballad, "The Three Fishers,"
for the singing of which, she evidently
desired to impress her listeners, she was
justly famed.

The mention of this pleasant homely
song sounded somewhat incongruous
upon the lips from which it was mo-
mentarily expected would issue the
ravishing notes of an operatic aria, but
then the comforting assurance of Chris-
tine Nilsson and her frequent rendition
of "Down upon the Swanee River"
rescued the mind of the hostess from
annoying doubts, and she asked her
siren if she felt equal to quieting the
feverish impatience of her guests, and
singing to them at once.

The songstress graciously acquiesced
without delay, and announced she would

give the famous duo from "Aida,"
first.

This was more than some of those
present had been led to expect, but it
was beyond any one's presumption to
inquire why she should undertake so
much at once. The hostess even feeling seriously annoyed with herself that
across her mental vision should pass the
remembrance of a concert given by the
colored waiters of a watering-place at
which she was stopping, and at which
the master of ceremonies had announced
that "Messrs. Smith, Jones and Rob-
inson, would sing a quarteeter." The
lionne of the evening further confided that she should be obliged to have
the front drawing-room cleared of
people, as she would like it entirely to
herself. This was accomplished, the
now wondering and awe-struck audience allowing themselves to be shoo'd
around in most docile fashion. Her final
request was for some "red drapery."

The eldest child of the house was hurriedly pressed into the conversation at this juncture, and upon being made to understand what was required, asked in a "stage whisper," "And must it be red?" Upon being assured that the color was imperative, she vouchsafed the information that the only red thing she knew of in the house was the shawl used to throw over the poll-parrot's cage at night.

She was sent rapidly in quest of the same, and, placed in the hands of the singer, it was used by her to wind and drape about her shoulders; the effect desired to be gained thereby having to be left much to the imagination of the beholders.

Finally the gas was lowered in the room now doing duty as the stage, to that mysterious light reckoned as romantic, and the future prima-donna struck the key-note on the piano; then, minus any further accompaniment, soared away into the intricacies of the promised duo.

But what was this ! A solo after all ? For, reaching the limits of her own part, she suddenly ceased singing, and threw herself into an attitude of expectancy (so did the audience).

It proved to be an interlude of complete silence during which the second voice was supposed to be taking up the theme.

Matters were conducted on this principle to the finish, when the lady strode toward the imaginary footlights, gave one final triumphant note, and fell flat on her back with her feet (which candor compelled the hostess to admit were not like "those little mice, etc.,") to the audience.

This was not recognized by all to be a dramatic climax, and, in their ignorance, they came hurriedly forward to "help her up," but others, less charitably inclined, perhaps, sought the

MAURICE BARRYMORE.

friendly shelter of a sofa-cushion, or a handkerchief, in which to bury their convulsed features.

The artiste needed no assistance, but sprang eagerly to her feet, seeking in all directions to ascertain the effect she had produced, especially upon some rather illustrious personages present ; but the hostess sought in turn to save her from the knowledge, by immediate offer of refreshment and almost of retirement. These were not accepted, however, and she became suddenly aware that, by some extraordinary means, the late exponent of " Aida " was occupying the piano-stool, and, with or without consent, was narrating to her already too highly amused guests the woes of " The Three Fishers."

A First Experience with a Busy Manager of Burlesque.

THREADING my way in and out among the crowds thronging Broadway one sunny morning in spring, I chanced upon a young authoress of my acquaintance, accompanied by her mother and her business manager. By mutual volition we stopped to exchange a few words, the authoress informing me with a touch of pride in her voice, that having written a burlesque, the outlines of which were already somewhat approved, they were on their way to keep an appointment, at his office, with the famous manager of that branch of the drama, Mr. Ed. E. Rice; adding an invitation to join them if I so desired.

Being possessed of sufficient desire to make acquaintance with my friend's latest work, as well as to note its effect upon Mr. Rice, I accepted the hastily proffered invitation, and we accordingly pursued our way through Thirtieth Street to the well-known office.

From the drift of her remarks, I felt assured the young woman was not fully prepared for the experience in store for her, and felt inclined to give utterance to some timely warning— but refrained. Having had her pathway prepared, she evidently expected to be ushered into a quiet, well-ordered apartment, where the manager would be anxiously awaiting her advent to tender her the full hour of audience which she had been promised, in which to discuss in a leisurely manner the *pros* and *cons* of the piece, and, without doubt in her own mind, Mr. Rice, at the close of the interview, would become the proud possessor of the treasured MS.

Knowing that in another moment

thé facts would probably speak for themselves, I held my peace, until our entrance into the office put a stop to all further confidences.

To the trained eye, the first glimpse of the room was sufficient to dispel the idea of a lengthened interview with any one individual, it being packed with the *genus* "variety," from the door to the screen half enclosing Mr. Rice's desk—each and all, eager to be the next to claim the managerial attention.

Indeed, it appeared as though the entire company of "1492" (the reigning burlesque attraction), including their friends, had dropped in for a morning chat.

It had not yet dawned upon our novice in ways burlesque, however, that the apparent state of affairs could in any way affect the business upon which she had come ; regarding the latter, so to speak, as a thing apart ; and thus she rested easily against the door while her man of business made his way forward to present his client's name.

Mr. Rice, rushingly busy as usual, dotting down memoranda, dictating to his type-writer at intervals, and answering "half a dozen questions at once," propounded by as many different people, stopped an instant, but scarce taking time to glance up, replied in his characteristic fashion—"All right, ask the lady to step this way."

This she did, preparatory, as she supposed, to being led into some retired spot away from this "madding crowd." The manager wheeling round in his chair as she made her appearance, nodded to her, remarking : "Miss —— I believe ? I shall have to ask you to tell me what you can of this——"

"What ! here ?" she gasped, with an astonishment that was pathetic.

"Yes," continued Mr. Rice, " I am sorry I cannot give you the hour I mentioned, but I had forgotten a re-
13

hearsal I have to superintend, that will
commence in about ten minutes." He
went on to suggest that, meanwhile,
half of that precious time was at her
disposal in which to present to him a
résumé of her burlesque, and a general
idea of the music ; the details he would
look into later on.

Having offered her the best opportunity in his power under the circumstances, he calmly surveyed the army
of his as yet unsatisfied visitors over
the top of the young lady's head, and
prepared to listen with that imperturb-
able manner born of necessity and
habit, to what she had to say, although
I am bound to state the facilities for
hearing were not augmented by the
chattering of the motley throng.

A veteran might have been equal
to the situation, and possibly scored a
success, but the young girl in question
was literally " struck dumb " by this
request to "state her case" within the

limit given, and amidst the din confusing her. She finally faltered out, "That it would be better for her to come upon another occasion, and—and——"

The manager bowed, wasted no time in remonstrance, and simply proceeded with the "next in turn."

The bewildered young woman, slipping from the room followed by her friends, made her way rapidly to the street, where they stopped and held a semi-indignation meeting, and for the moment I fear scarcely appreciated my remark, that though the little encounter had scarcely been of an agreeable nature to them, at the same time they must appreciate the fact that Mr. Rice, though but one single individual, evidently found it necessary to attempt the work of six, and, therefore, with the very best intentions, could not fail to encounter difficulties in trying to fulfil and meet the requirements of all.

Jottings.

It is curious to note the evolution of
the wheel of fortune, the rotations of
which can perhaps be followed more
clearly in the dramatic profession than
any other, for the reason that their lives
are more *en evidence* than those whose
affairs force them less before the public.

Years ago when the " Star Theatre "
was not the " Star," but " Wallack's,"
and considered as well the most fashionable place of amusement in the city,
Lester Wallack was regarded as the
head and front of theatrical management, the handsomest actor on the
stage, and one of the most elegant men
about town. He rarely walked a block
in the street that he was not privately
as well as openly followed by admiring

femininity, his picture probably adorned
the dressing-table of nearly every girl
in town, and being of good English
family, as well as a man of charmingly
cultivated intellect and taste, his *prestige* in every way was unquestioned,
making the history of his life that of
success and pleasure unrivalled.

He simply coined money, both at his
own theatre and throughout the country ; "Wallack's yacht," "country
houses," "coach," and all that attend
upon such luxuries, were discussed, but
at the same time, to a certain extent,
taken as a matter of course.

The receipts poured in so naturally,
so ceaselessly, that little wonder it never
occurred to this favored being that any
other condition of affairs was possible.
At the time of his greatest opulence
Theodore Moss was in Wallack's em-
ploy. The former was plodding and
methodical, and he gradually became
very useful to the brilliant actor, who

left the arrangement of business details more and more in his hands. To give some idea of the amount of money that Mr. Wallack had at his command, he bought a yacht and a house at Long Branch one year, for which he paid, cash down, ninety thousand dollars; but, though his capacity for making money seemed unlimited, his capacity for business was *nil.*

The only instance on record of his being extremely cautious, was when visiting Budd's furnishing store one day in company with one of his sons, when, after having given an order for two or three hundred dollars' worth of goods, and handing in his check for the same, he remarked: "Now, Budd, I want a receipt for this, if you please." His son laughingly tried to convince him that the witnesses to the transaction, and his own check and stub would be a sufficient guarantee against any trouble that possibly might arise in the

future, but Mr. Wallack gravely per-
sisted in having the receipt.

As a contrast to the above, he would
certify checks, leaving the amount blank
for Mr. Moss to fill in ; the latter could
then at any time have made one out
for every cent Mr. Wallack was worth.
Monies were also put in the bank under
the name of Moss to save Mr. Wallack
the trouble of making his own deposits.

This almost culpable carelessness
could lead to but one result : the Thirtieth Street theatre was built under his
supervision, but from that time on,
matters went from bad to worse, one
piece of property after another was
sold to meet demands which in some
way never could be satisfied, and the
end ?

Mr. Wallack died, a few years since,
a comparatively poor man.

*   *   *   *   *

Mr. A. M. Palmer, who shares with

Mr. Augustin Daly the leading managerial honors of to-day, strikes one as
another instance of reversing the original order of things.

In earlier days he held the post of
Librarian of the "Mercantile Library,"
then, as now, located in Astor Place.

Later on, be became interested in
various matters with Mr. Sheridan
Shook, manager of what had become
the famous "Union Square Theatre ;"
justly so, because of its magnificent
stock-company, fine selection of plays,
and the manner in which the same
were presented to the public.

The relations of Shook and Palmer
became more consolidated as time went
on, until, as is sometimes the case in a
close race, when the bystanders notice
the nose of the rear horse creep up and
shoot by the leader, until, to return to
the men in question, the name of A. M.
Palmer stood alone as that of winner,
and Mr. Shook was — well, I don't ex-

actly know where, but justly, however, "to the victor belongs the spoils."

To those who regard a prominent manager's judgment of a play, after reading it, as infallible, it will be surprising to know that Mr. Palmer is quoted as saying he has about concluded that it is somewhat in the light of an impossibility to predict what might, or might not, be a success with the public, until after the curtain has been rung down on the first representation, and a few weeks later this utterance was verified in the following manner.

At an entertainment to be given at his theatre two one-act plays were to make up a portion of the programme, a tragedy and a comedy.

After perusing both, Mr. Palmer dropped the tragedy MS. on the table before him, remarking, "I don't think anything of that, but this," referring to the comedy, "is good, and will succeed." His verdict was promptly reversed, three weeks after, by the audience before whom the plays were given, and by the newspaper accounts the following morning.

The tragedy held the people breathless, and called forth exhaustive criticism from the press, while the comedy was merely mentioned as having been given a place on the programme.

*　　*　　*　　*　　*

Augustin Daly—regarded as the great disciplinarian manager—is so respected, feared and omnipresent with his company that in the old days at least of his reign over them, at the "Fifth Avenue Theatre," he was often referred to by the less reverent members of his troupe as "God," some even going so far as to kneel daily on the mat outside the closed door of his private room in the play-house, and offer up prayers.

The fact that he made it a rule not to notice the members of his company outside the theatre was a matter of sore speculation with some, and certainly did not meet their approval. Mr. Louis James proving to be one of these. Soon after being engaged by Mr. Daly, he met him and his brother, Judge Daly, on the street; not knowing of the above rule, he bowed to them both ; the judge recognized Mr. James, but the manager did not, and it then became a sort of " war-to-the-knife " feeling with the actor, so much so that, during the three years he remained under him, he never spoke to the manager except in the way of business, and, I fear, despite the value of his services, in a quiet way made himself somewhat of a thorn in the managerial flesh. Miss Fanny Davenport and Mr. James had made their appearance in public somewhere about the same period at Mrs. Drew's theatre in Philadelphia, and,

happening to become good friends, it
naturally followed when they found
themselves together in Mr. Daly's company that their good fellowship so to
speak, should continue. Thus in the
intervals of rehearsal, or between acts,
they indulged in many a gay chat,
sometimes standing by the door of Miss
Davenport's dressing-room, sometimes
elsewhere.

This evidently caused the manager
displeasure, as ere long a notice was
posted up to the effect, "That any
of the ladies or gentlemen of the company found conversing in the neighbor-
hood of the dressing-rooms, or during
the progress of a performance, would
be fined," so much. Mr. James' dressing-room at that time happened to
be directly over Miss Davenport's, with
one large window extending through
both, so, after the notice appeared, as a
mild form of revenge and annoyance,
the actor and actress indulged in un-

usually lengthy confabs, using the window as a means of communication.

On another occasion during the rehearsal of a play which had been placed "under the ban" by the whole company, and when they thought themselves alone, the body of the theatre being shrouded in extreme darkness, Mr. James had just finished a stilted scene, which to express his contempt of, he gave a sort of "Flowers-of-Spring" hop, tra la, as he made his exit—but was surprised to hear himself suddenly recalled by a stern and uncompromising voice that seemed to arise from the apparently untenanted orchestra.

"Mr. James."

Reappearing on the stage, and looking in the direction from which the voice emanated—Mr. James answered quickly, "Yes, sir."

"Do you intend," continued the voice, "to use that piece of business in which you have just indulged in your part, when presenting it before the public?"

Mr. James replied in an equally impressive tone: "I really don't know, Mr. Daly, I haven't quite decided the matter as yet."

Notwithstanding peculiarities, Mr. Daly's policy has proved a good one, for the years come and go, only to find him mounting higher and higher the ladder of success and prosperity, and to realize that his name is a power on both sides of the Atlantic.

*　　*　　*　　*　　*

Miss Ada Rehan, Daly's present "leading lady," represents a striking example of the limitless good fortune that may be attained by a woman possessed of talent and perseverance.

Who, to contemplate this peerless creature, can imagine that her life has ever been otherwise than it is at present! And yet it has been different, more to her credit be it said.

Among the guests of a theatre party visiting "Daly's" one evening was a very charming Irishman, a well-known man about town. As Miss Rehan made her exit, at the finish of the first act of the piece being presented, amidst the vociferous applause of the large audience present, the gentleman emitted a little sigh of satisfaction, remarking softly, "Well, well, it is difficult to realize that little Biddy and the queenly Ada are the same."

Upon being pressed for an explanation of this, he confided the fact to his friends, that when his father was alive and living in Ireland, "Biddy," as he called her, with other children, ran barefoot over the estate.

It is a wonderful thing to realize how Miss Rehan has worked her way up patiently, step by step, until she has reached the first position. Truly, a magnificent example of courage.

*   *   *   *   *

Mr. Charles Hoyt, the phenomenally successful manager and author from New Hampshire, has ever a dry, humorous, unpretentious manner of regarding matters, and apparently himself included.

A young playwright was transacting some business with Mr. Charles W. Thomas, the late partner of Mr. Hoyt, in their joint office one morning, when the latter came in. After a little desultory conversation, the author said, "Mr. Hoyt, what is one to do ? Give me your advice, for, having been so successful, you can afford to." Mr. Hoyt inquired upon what subject, and the young woman replied, "Well, my plays are acknowledged to be good by any number of critics, and yet the market seems so overstocked it is almost an impossibility to obtain a production for them."

Mr. Hoyt replied briskly: "Well, I don't know that I can be of any service to you, for the cases are different. No one ever took any particular notice of the plays I wrote, until I just hired my own theatre and brought them out myself."

The result of Mr. Hoyt's policy requires no comment.

*   *   *   *   *

Peculiar coincidences come to light now and then in the profession, leaving the participants thereof a prey to certain superstitious feelings.

Several years since, a burlesque was written for an amateur troupe of young men; the author of the same being especially admonished to create a particularly "fat part," for one of the members, Mr. James K. Hackett, who was considered by many to dis-
14

tance any of the performers belonging
to the "Columbia Dramatic" organization; but, as the latter would not admit
that such was the case, the young
aspirant for amateur dramatic honor
(then studying to be admitted to the
bar) was to be given this opportunity to
demonstrate the fact beyond a question.

The performance was given, and the
rôle allotted to Mr. Hackett was of a
dashing, brilliant order, in which he
realized the fondest hopes of his cham-
pions ; indeed, he made an unqualified
success of it. This fact naturally impressed him with friendly feeling towards the author of the piece. Two years
passed, however, and neither of them
had met. The latter had been told, or
been given to understand in some vague
way that the young man who burlesqued
Carmencita's dancing so wonderfully
had abandoned the study of law and
entered the theatrical profession ; but

one morning about this time, while two
of her short plays were in course of
rehearsal at "Palmer's Theatre," happening to glance up, she saw Mr.
Hackett making his way on from the
wings.   After the ordinary greetings
the playwright inquired, "And what
brings you here ?"

"The very question I was going to pro-
pound to you," replied the young actor.

"Why, I am watching the rehearsal
of two of my pieces," she answered.

"And I have been sent to take a
small part in one or other of them," he
responded, "though I did not know they
were yours."

Mutual explanations followed, and
later on, when the "leading man" engaged for one of the plays failed to
appear, Mr. Hackett was given the
position and thus made his professional *début* in a character of any importance in a play by the same author
as that of the burlesque.   Making

a success of it he was now inspired
with a certain superstition in regard to
her work, and some months later he
arranged to tour a part of the country
in another of her pieces.   He made considerable reputation for himself in this,
and the author is now to write a play
to order for him, of which he hopes to
make a notable production.

*   *   *   *   *

Lotta, the sprightly little creature of
whom the public was so fond, has left a
great gap by withdrawing herself from
the boards of late, let us hope not per-
manently.   Notwithstanding her great
popularity, I remember her vacation
life at Lake George—when she hired a
little cottage two or three miles down
the lake from the "Fort William
Henry Hotel—" was simplicity itself.
There she remained the whole summer through with the members of her

family, and an occasional friend to visit them.

With her fine auburn hair hanging down her back in large soft curls, and a muslin slip-dress on, she looked little more than a child ; and her chief delight was to find some one who would play croquet with her, which game she would indulge in as long as there was a partner to be had.

One day, while discussing matters theatrical, she observed it was wonderful the trifles that could disturb her part in a play, unless they happened to be just so.

In one piece, a portion of her costume consisted of an old sunbonnet, which she was in the habit of pulling and shoving all over her head during her scene, and she declared she became so dependent upon it, that had it been missing at any time, she veritably believed she should not have been able to get through with her part, for she had experienced something of the same description in another play. It was one in which she dressed as a boy, and her greatest comfort while in this garb was to thrust her hands into her trousers' pockets.

Her mother had remonstrated with her in vain for doing this, but to no avail, so, without apprising her daughter of the fact, Mrs. Crabtree sewed the pockets up one fine day.

The same night, when Lotta came bounding on to the stage, and her hands sought their usual resting-place, they sought in vain, and consternation claimed the little actress for its own. In fact, so thoroughly did this altera-tion upset her that she completely forgot her part for the time being, and did not regain her equilibrium until the scissors were brought into play, and ripped up the mischief done.

* * * * *

Mr. Barnabee, the genial and dignified "Sheriff of Nottingham," in De
Koven's opera of "Robin Hood," and
third part proprietor of the organization
known as the "Bostonians," according to
his own showing, made a very modest
beginning of his theatrical career.

When quite a young man he was employed in the dry-goods store of a well-
known Boston merchant, and he, with
some young men of his accquaintance
having aspirations of their own, organized a dramatic club for diversion in
the evenings, indulging in anything
theatrical their fancy dictated.

He had been for some time employed
in the store, but had never as yet encountered the proprietor, who was
popularly supposed to be a somewhat
austere person ; therefore, when one
morning he was suddenly summoned to
his presence in the latter's private office,
the young clerk's heart felt anything
but normal in its workings, and his

mind searched vainly to discern in what he had been derelict, for he could not imagine the summons portended anything less than dismissal.

His employer commenced the interview by telling him that the evening before he had witnessed an amateur performance in which he had recognized him, Barnabee, as taking part. The latter's spirits now sank to zero, feeling positive he detected signs of disapproval in the tones of the former ; what was his surprise, however, at the unexpected ending.

"Now," continued the gentleman, "my wife and family being away in the country, I am proposing to give a 'stag' dinner, at which I desire all the guests shall personate an especial character. I thought your acting proved you to be especially clever in dialect Yankee parts, and I should like you to attend the repast as my down-east country cousin."

The relief occasioned by the purport of this interview was of course very great, and Mr. Barnabee made haste to accept the invitation extended.

The dinner proved a great success, the various characters all being well portrayed, and it was, in consequence, productive of much mirth.

After this, one circumstance led to another, until Mr. Barnabee realized the dry-goods store was a thing of the past, and the stage his profession.

Napoleon, Lover and Husband

By FREDERIC MASSON

Translated from the 14th French Edition
By J. M. HOWELL

FIVE PHOTOGRAVURE PLATES, 320 PAGES, 8VO, CLOTH, GILT TOP, $2.00

* * * Frederic Masson has undertaken to reveal the lover's side, as it may be called, of Napoleon, from the precocious youth to the day that he died at St. Helena. The book is what might be called a "revelation," for, though many of the names and episodes treated have been vaguely touched before, the present author has buttressed his statements by documents which a court of law would be compelled to pronounce unimpeachable. And, indeed, without documents, the Napoleon presented in Frederic Masson's volume, "Napoleon, Lover and Husband," would be hardly credible, for, if there is one saliency in Napoleon's character that stands out beyond others in the recorded actions of his life, it is his determined hostility to feminine interference in affairs of state, or even affairs of the family. It was his supposed impassive indifference to the sex that first won him the incredulous interest of the Parisians, when, as the head of the Italian army at twenty-five, he sternly put aside the usual gallantries that follow "war's alarms," and found time only for conjugal letters to the absent Josephine.

* * * Paris, and indeed all Europe, seems to be struck with the remarkable recrudescence of the Napoleonic legends. Not only are plays reviving the career of Napoleon presented on two or three of the Parisian stages simultaneously, but half the national periodicals are deep in new "studies" of the extinct volcano. Masson's book, which, it is no exaggeration to say, is exciting a sensation from St. Petersburg to Rome, derives its chief force from the fact that the revelations are drawn from friendly sources, and the writer presents the result rather in the spirit of a philosophic and admiring friend than a severe censor of morals or a critic of character.

For sale at all Bookstores, or will be mailed postpaid upon receipt of price by

THE MERRIAM COMPANY

67 Fifth Avenue   New York

MY UNCLE BENJAMIN

A HUMOROUS AND • • • •
• • PHILOSOPHICAL NOVEL

::: BY :::

CLAUDE TILLIER

ILLUSTRATED, 12MO, CLOTH, $1.25

A novel unlike any other, by an author unlike any other; a
novel that has no equivalent in the literature of this century;
a novel which, despite the pessimism with which it opens and the
pathos with which it closes, must take rank among the wittiest
and most humorous ever written; a novel of philosophy, of progress, of reality, of humanity; a novel of the heart and of the
head; a novel which is less a work of art than a work of genius.

PRESS NOTICES

The Brooklyn Eagle says: "This book is a production
worthy to take rank with the best of Fielding's, Smollett's,
Richardson's, Marryatt's, or any of the old English novels, for
its hearty, healthy sense and sentiment and its sound or curious
characters."

The Boston Post says: "It is a pessimistic and sombre story,
but not without a strong charm of human sympathy and interest,
and relieved by the ready wit and a finely flavored humor that
touches upon the philosophical."

The Chicago Figaro says: "How can one better describe a
favorite book than by acknowledging that in finishing the last
chapter one feels as if an old friend were gone? It is this feeling
which we have in closing the covers of ' My Uncle Benjamin.' "

The Merriam Company
Publishers and Booksellers
67 Fifth Avenue   *New York*

Broadoaks...

A Delightful Story of Virginian Life

—BY—

M. G. McClelland

ILLUSTRATED BY CHARLES EDWARD BOUTWOOD

12mo, Cloth, $1.00

This is one of the most delightful stories that ever flowed from the facile pen of this author. As a story of the South—for the South is Miss McClelland's favorite *locale*—it should take high rank and with commensurate popularity, for Southern stories have a charm all their own—a charm so indefinable and elusive that it cannot be analyzed. Few authors write well of the South. It requires an especial faculty not often possessed. Northern types and traits may be treated sketchily, after the snapshot system; but when one takes up one's pen to write of the paradise that lies below Mason and Dixon's line one must necessarily be imbued with sympathy, sentiment, something of the inborn poesy of nature, else one's work will be neither effective, natural, nor artistic. There is throughout the book that delicacy of touch which betrays the finer instinct; that graphic quality of description which suggests knowledge and acquaintance, and that occasional tenderness of treatment which tells its own story. "Broadoaks" is a strong creation, one that will add materially to its author's already widespread national fame.

For sale by all Booksellers, or will be sent post-paid on receipt of price by

The Merriam Company

67 FIFTH AVENUE   **NEW YORK**

A Common Mistake,

The Story of a New

York Society Girl .

BY

Jeanne M. Howell

12mo, Cloth, 50 Cts.

Sylvia Gilchrist is an epitome of the undisciplined, brilliant, nervous young womanhood of America. Gifted with an exceptionally fine physique and of bright mind, she only knows her power to wield it capriciously and of her own sweet will. The book is delightful, and every trunk packed for seashore or mountain should contain a copy.

PRESS NOTICES

The New York *Morning Journal* says: "This is a story distinctly superior to three-fourths of the fiction that is poured in a flood upon the counters of the booksellers."

The Boston *Traveller* says: "It is one of the best novels of the season."

The Chicago *Saturday Evening Herald* says: "This novel is a decidedly clever piece of work."

The Grand Rapids *Review* says: " . . . It is more than a fascinating story. It is a study, and a careful study, of that most delightful, but little understood, creature, the 'society girl.'"

For sale by all Booksellers, or will be sent post-paid on receipt of price by

The Merriam Company

Publishers and Booksellers

67 Fifth Avenue   *New York*

LINGUA GEMMAE ∴

A Cycle of Gems by ADA L. SUTTON

Profusely Illustrated by Mary Fairman Clark. 16mo, Cloth, Gilt Top, $1.50

THIS little book is the most complete thing of the kind ever published. It comprises a description of one hundred precious stones, with their poetic selections, properties, localities, and sentiments, and the explanations are clear, concise and comprehensive, and as a Hand-Book of Precious Gems the book will be invaluable to jewellers and lapidaries.

The poems have been selected from the most popular poets of the day, and with its dainty binding and attractive illustrations, LINGUA GEMMÆ will prove one of the most tempting gift-books published for the holidays.

Belle-Plante • and • Cornelius

.. BY ..

CLAUDE TILLIER
Author of "My Uncle Benjamin"

ILLUSTRATED, 12MO, CLOTH, $1.25

One cannot have too much of Claude Tillier. He stands forth in bold relief as an eloquent example of the rugged, honest style of the past, made more effective by virtue of contrast with the conventional, artificial style of to-day. He appeals to us with an old gospel newly interpreted—the gospel of humanity. He calls a spade a spade, and speaks from the heart. Others have done the former, but so few, comparatively speaking, have done the latter that Tillier is almost unique.

As a story "Belle-Plante and Cornelius" may not have the direct human interest of "My Uncle Benjamin"; but, as a keen and sympathetic study of the fair ideal and the bald real, of the higher and baser instincts of man, of the diversity of types, of the compensations of genius, and of the charms of the muck-rake, it ranks far above the other book. Belle-Plante and his brother, Cornelius, are as undeniable types of to-day and of every age as are Dives and Lazarus. Belle-Plante represents the spirit of greed which nurses the real because of its intrinsic value as a marketable commodity. Cornelius stands for the Sisyphus who toils up the slope which leads to the height of fame, hampered at every step, strained at every point, and frequently borne backward by the weight of the commonplace. Belle-Plante is the plodder, Cornelius is the poet. Belle-Plante is the world, which exacts every farthing of tribute ere it will listen to the dreaming Cornelius. Belle-Plante is humanity, which steals the fruits of genius and leaves Cornelius penniless. Cornelius is Tillier, but slightly idealized, while Belle-Plante is the ill fortune which robbed the world of a philosopher. In refusing to give his brother meat and drink, Belle-Plante merely gives the highest expression to commercial benevolence.

The Merriam Company
Publishers and Booksellers

67 Fifth Avenue   **New York**